'SHE'S GONNA BLOW!'

Even as the last spray of spittle hit Waring in the
face, the cap exploded and the gusher roared
forty feet high. Then it dropped for a moment
and spurted again, higher this time, drenching
them in a warm, clear liquid.

Rob was the first to react. At that moment he
realised why he was made of executive material.
It was all to do with foresight and quick
reactions. He grabbed Ben's arm and pulled him
a few yards to one side, away from prying ears.

And when he spoke his voice was staccato and
authoritative.

'I want this site sealed. I want this fence fixed
and I want signed affidavits from all personnel
that if they breathe a word of this, we'll have
their ass.'

'Why, for Chrissake?' said Ben.

'Because,' Rob whispered, 'we've struck friggin'
mineral water.'

Water

GORDON McGILL

A novelisation based on the screenplay
by **DICK CLEMENT** and
IAN LA FRENAIS and
BILL PERSKY

Story by **BILL PERSKY**

SPHERE BOOKS LIMITED
London and Sydney

First published in Great Britain by
Sphere Books Ltd 1985
30-32 Gray's Inn Road, London WC1X 8JL
Copyright © 1985 by Gordon McGill

FREEDOM: Music by Eric Clapton, lyrics by
    Eric Clapton and Ian La Frenais © 1984
    E.C. Music Ltd

CASCARA: Music by Mike Moran, lyrics by Ian La
    Frenais, sung by Lance Ellington © 1984
    Ganga Publishing BV

CASCARAN NATIONAL ANTHEM, LISTEN TO MY
    SONG and BLACK GOLD: Music by Mike Moran, lyrics
    by Dick Clement, Ian La Frenais and Bill Persky
    © 1984 Ganga Publishing BV

TRADE
MARK

Set in Century

Printed and bound in Great Britain by
Cox & Wyman Ltd, Reading

Water

Preface

Delgado Fitzhugh had lain awake all night, impatiently waiting for the dawn. Every few minutes he had touched one of the grenades on the pillow or run his fingers along the bandoleer hanging from a nail on the wall, fluttering his fingertips against the bullets, playing imaginary music as if it were the neck of a guitar.

He was naked except for the black Castro beret covering his privacy. His combat fatigues hung on the back of the door, hardly visible in the dark, camouflaged to merge with the Cascaran bush. Mosquitoes whined but he paid them no attention. Fidel had never worried about such irrelevancies as insects and nor would he.

On the floor Garfield snored gently and Delgado envied him his tranquillity, but then, Garfield was only number two. He did not have the responsibility.

Again, for the twentieth time, he practised the words and polished the phrasing, getting it right, well aware that what he had to say would be recorded and would go down in history. All his life, however long that was, he had waited for this day and now he was ready. The time had come to put theory into practice.

The sun was late, held back by banks of cumulus, but as soon as it broke through, Delgado leapt off the bunk and prodded Garfield, who came slowly awake, grunting oaths. Delgado silenced him with a finger on his lips, then quickly dressed; first the fatigues, then the Guevara headband and the Castro beret, then the ammunition and the boots.

When they were ready, Delgado tapped his fingers on the radio which was emitting a low whine. Like all

Cascarans, he kept the radio on at night thinking that the hum kept away mosquitoes. Jay Jay the Dee Jay would soon be coming on the air and the people would listen to him. There were not many possessions on the island but every house had a radio. Delgado was well aware of the fact and intended to make use of it.

He picked up his guitar, painted in camouflage colours like his fatigues, waited while Garfield slung his Kalashnikov over his shoulder, then they left the shack, went out into the heat of the morning without breakfast in the belief that hunger sharpened the senses, moving unseen through the bush, only their berets sharply outlined against the undergrowth and the words lovingly stitched in black on their shoulders: CASCARAN LIBERATION FRONT.

As he moved towards his destiny, Delgado was proud to be who he was. Already he could see himself being welcomed in Havana and Moscow, and the thought of Moscow made him shiver, for he had spent all his life in the Caribbean and could not conceive of the cold.

One

Sunlight zipped through Jay Jay's shutters, casting a zebra pattern on the bunk. Slowly he awoke, eased himself to his feet and checked his appearance in the cracked mirror. Some of the dreadlocks had escaped in the night. He tucked them under his Rasta hat, yawned, put on his sunglasses, reached for the rum bottle, gargled the sleep from his throat and spat out into the washbasin.

The room was eight feet square, a jumble of records, tapes and posters, a filing cabinet, tape deck and console and Jay Jay's swing chair by the window. Jay Jay sat, swung to his left and threw the shutters open. The shack, with the letters 'Radio Cascara' scrawled on the wall, was the highest building on the island, half hidden in foliage, standing a hundred and fifty feet above the town.

From his window Jay Jay could see the whole of Port Agnes, the six streets and the square, every corrugated tin roof, almost every doorway down to the jetty in the east and the church in the west. Only Government House, a mile to the north, was hidden from view and Jay Jay, being a curious man, resented the Governor's privacy.

The town hummed with the sound of a hundred radios and Jay Jay snapped his fingers, slipped a tape into the deck and grinned, a mouthful of yellow teeth splitting the shiny black face. It was time for them to wake up.

He hit a button and Port Agnes throbbed to the sound of reggae. Jay Jay checked his watch and leant into the mike.

'Toots and the Maytalls,' he crooned, 'bringing us to

3

seven thirty-five here on Radio Cascara, your station of the stars. This is Jay Jay Johnstone, in the seat and on the beat.'

He spun round, picked up a pair of binoculars and scanned the scene below, saw young Winston doing wheelies on an ancient bicycle towards the square, where old Paco was gathering up bottles from the night before and dropping them in his dustcart.

Swinging to the right, he focused on the old church, paint peeling, roof in disrepair and the sign: 'St Marks Presbyterian Church, Port Agnes. Rev. Eric McNab, Pastor.'

The door opened and the Reverend squinted into the sun, his face an explosion of broken capillaries, then he rubbed his hands over three days of stubble.

Jay Jay nodded and sat back, swinging round to the sound of the Maytalls, a happy man with his finger on the pulse of the community.

Eric McNab grunted as he struggled up the hill towards Radio Cascara. He was uncomfortable. The gradient made his heart flutter and the sound of reggae assaulted his brain. In all his thirty-odd years on the island, he had never got accustomed to calypso, funji or reggae. He was more of a Jimmy Shand man himself.

Nor had he ever been able to adjust to the heat, and that morning he was fondly reminiscing about the Glasgow drizzle and coal fires in the range. Briefly he stopped and loosened the dog collar still further until it dropped onto his chest. Like a cow looking over a dyke, his old father would have said.

Feeling old, hungover and homesick, he dragged himself up the crumbling wooden steps towards Jay Jay's door, paused for a moment to catch his breath then pushed it open.

Jay Jay waved at him as he talked into the mike.

'Coming up at eight o'clock,' he said, 'The BBC World News, and before that the Reverend Eric McNab with his thought for the day.'

4

McNab did not react, just stumbled past him to the filing cabinet and grabbed the rum bottle. First things first. There were priorities to be observed. He picked up a mug, upturned it, grimaced, cleaned it with the tail of his shirt, poured himself a stiff one and gulped it down.

'But first the weather,' said Jay Jay. 'It's gonna be another hot one.'

The wind blasted through the shutters, pinning the old man to the cabinet and fluttering papers.

'Hot and windy,' said Jay Jay. 'Just like always.'

He turned and peered at the town through his binoculars, holding onto his hat with his free hand. In the square the sudden squall had scattered old Paco's garbage, and across the road a donkey reared up in fright. Someone was in trouble.

'Uh-oh,' said Jay Jay. 'Traffic news.'

Quickly he palmed a jingle into the deck, waited for it to finish, then bent once more to the mike.

'If you're driving to work, try to avoid Princess Elizabeth Street where T-Bone Jefferson's truck has just shed a load of mangoes.'

Then he winked at McNab and grinned. Promised to be a busy day, he thought.

A mile to the north, Baxter Thwaites watered his plants and took a long hit from a home-made cigar, the tobacco wrapped in paper torn from the leader in the *Times*. It was the best time of day, before the wind became too strong and the sun too hot and while most of the biting bugs were still asleep.

Baxter was in philosophical mood, thinking about contentment. He wasn't exactly happy, he told the plants. Happiness was something positive, whereas contentment was passive. He nodded and smiled, pleased with the idea; and yet, once upon a time, things had been different, when he had been fuelled with ambition. In the early days, after university, there seemed to be no limit to his potential. He had all the credentials for a brilliant career in the Foreign and Commonwealth Service, but somehow

5

it hadn't worked out. A series of postings in Latin America had led to Cascara. At the time he was the youngest Governor in the Caribbean – fifteen years ago when he was not yet thirty.

For a while he had deluded himself that the island had some importance. Whitehall had wittered on about Cuba being interested in the harbour. There had been some talk of the Americans being leased a few acres to build a tracking station, but it was all nonsense. Cascara was nothing more than a piece of volcanic rock between St Lucia and Martinique; thirteen miles of slag heap, its only feature being the volcano which grumbled constantly like an appendix and regularly showered the island with black dust.

There was no beach. The sea was a cauldron of jellyfish and sharks. There were scorpions and fer-de-lance in the bush and no one in the port with whom one could have a conversation of more than three syllables, except for the Reverend McNab, when he was sober.

Cascara, Baxter had once said, was the runt of the Windwards' litter and should have been drowned at birth; and yet, in the early morning, a man without ambition could be content, almost glad to be alive in fact; content as a cud-chewing cow was content, or a pig in shit. Again Baxter grinned to himself and took a long pull from his cigar. Nature always had her compensations and, in the case of Cascara, it was the best ganja in the Caribbean.

A rustling in the bushes made him turn. A cultured voice called out: 'Gahvnah...'

He could hear Eddy Grant on the radio and he swayed to the rhythm, his Hawaiin shirt flapping outside the baggy khaki shorts, and he grinned beneath his New York Mets baseball cap; a large heavy man, slightly thick in the paunch and with a smile that made friends.

'I'm over here, Pepito,' he said. 'Enjoying the fruits of my labours.'

Two men pushed through the bushes and stopped: the brothers Smith, Nado and Pepito. Nado was the younger and carried a silver tray with the Governor's breakfast – a

6

pot of tea, cup and saucer, silver milk jug and toast rack with four pieces of toast and a jar of Frank Cooper's marmalade.

Nado offered it with a smile. He had no discernible ambition other than to be a good servant in Government House and work as few hours as possible.

Pepito had inherited their mother's cunning and had taken elocution lessons in order to sound like someone from Weybridge. One of these days, he planned to see something of the world, using, as he put it, the coat-tails of the boss.

The boss was smiling at them now and clutching a watering can.

Pepito glanced at it and took his cue.

'It looks as though we'll have some splendid pineapples this year, Governor.'

Baxter shook his head and presented the cigar.

'Never mind the pineapples, old sport,' he said. 'Wrap your lips around this.'

Pepito took it, inhaled deeply and closed his eyes, holding in the smoke for as long as possible.

'I took a bit of a gamble,' said Baxter, 'crossing Bocachica with Bolivian Red Leaf.'

Pepito exhaled and nodded. 'Possibly as promising as the seventy-nine,' he said, handing it to his brother. There was a moment's silence as Nado took a hit. Baxter leant forward, frowning slightly, waiting for the verdict. Of the three of them, Nado was the connoisseur. As the young man closed his eyes, Baxter was reminded of the old days, the wine tastings in cellars in the City; red noses and sand buckets as spittoons. Nado would have been confused by the buckets.

At last he opened his eyes and grinned, and when he spoke, it was in the slow, fractured drawl of the true Cascaran.

'These are heavy-duty herbs, boss.'

And the Governor smiled, basking in his servant's approval...

After breakfast in the ganja patch, Baxter wandered

through the garden towards the house. It was the only building of any style on the island. A banana planter had built it in 1902. It had four bedrooms, a porch and an acre of ground. Some day, Baxter thought as he made his way beneath the flag-pole where the Union Jack was being blasted by the wind and between the two ancient cannons, the house would need a coat of paint. Maybe next autumn, perhaps.

Whistling softly, he wandered into the reception room. The place made him feel comfortable. It was lived-in and friendly with its ship's wheel by the window, the two rudders, the ship's bell and the figurehead leaning from the roof. She had lost her nose and one breast in the wreck but her smile remained. Baxter was fond of her.

The radio was playing the Wailers now and Baxter sang along as he reached his desk, then he stopped as the music was interrupted by a dreadful splintering noise, the sound of timber being smashed, and Baxter thought he heard a pained cry in a dreadfully familiar voice.

He switched up the volume and strained to hear what was going on. Over the sound of the Wailers he could hear voices, Jay Jay asking what was happening, then a grunt and the voice of an outraged Eric McNab, saying something about somebody having taken leave of their senses.

Then a moment of silence and Baxter nervously peered through the window towards the volcano. The last time Jay Jay went off the air was when the volcano erupted. But Mount Pestilence was quiet. He stood confused, head cocked like a bird, waiting, then staggered back as the room was blasted with noise.

'THIS IS THE VOICE OF RADIO FREE CASCARA!'

Baxter winced. He recognised the voice. It was Garfield Cooper and he was a nuisance. Then he heard Jay Jay muttering, 'Don't yell, man, you'll blow the transmitter.'

'Sorry,' said Garfield as he cleared his throat to make his announcement. 'Hear the voice of your leader, the Singing Rebel.'

8

'Oh bugger,' said Baxter as the room echoed to the discordant twang of a guitar accompanied by an electronic keyboard.

'*Brave Cascarans wherever you are,*' sang Delgado. The voice was guttural, a series of Glaswegian grunts, out of tune, fracturing the morning:

'*Listen please to my song.*'

Baxter's contentment evaporated into irritation. As he rushed upstairs to the bedroom, Delgado's song followed him.

'*Time to get rid of Colonial Oppressor*
Give back the Island where it belongs...'

Baxter burst into the bedroom and threw open the shutters, wrinkling his nose. The smell of cheap scent made him gag and the room, as always, reminded him of a cheap brothel. The walls were painted maroon. A chandelier tinkled in the wind. The dressing table was a jumble of bottles and jars. A box of chocolates lay on the bedside table on top of a copy of *Vogue*. On the bed Dolores sat up angrily, thrust aside the mosquito net and glared at him.

She seemed to Baxter to be slightly fatter than the night before, her make-up smeared, mascara running. Her fists pushed into the sheets compressed her cleavage – which seemed, in Baxter's imagination, to sneer at him. Even her tits, he thought, looked angry. She was wearing the red Janet Reger and some kind of jade necklace. All she needed, he thought, was a hat with fruit on it to make the picture complete.

'*Too long we suffer Imperialistic rule*
Too long our people Capitalist tool,' sang Delgado.

'Wha har you doing?' She snarled and again Baxter winced, recognising garlic, tequila and cheroot smoke. The voice, which he had once considered huskily Latin, now sounded like Louis Armstrong.

'Har you crazeee?' she asked.

Baxter smiled his supercilious smile as he pulled on a clean shirt.

9

'Sorry to disturb your beauty sleep, Dolores, but we have a crisis on our hands.'

'It's up to you to make a choice
Let me be your leader
Let me be your voice...'

Baxter cocked his head towards the radio. 'It's Delgado,' he said. 'He's never gone this far before.'

Dolores shrugged, freeing her breasts. They dropped and swayed to Delgado's rhythm.

'For thees you wheck me?'

'Yes, I know. It's terribly inconsiderate,' said Baxter, 'but if I'm going to subdue a revolution, I rather think I should wear my best trousers.' He smiled again. 'Have you seen my shoe?'

She had. She picked it up and hurled it at him, missing her target, shattering glass behind him.

Baxter's smile remained in place. He had had plenty of practice in remaining calm under fire but, just occasionally, Dolores' temperament got a tiny bit tedious.

'Thank you, darling,' he said, picked up the shoe and hopped out of the room.

The town throbbed to Delgado's message and the Cascarans idly took notice of it. Heads poked out of windows and people shuffled out of doorways. A group of women in the square swayed in rhythm and a bunch of kids practised kung fu kicks to the beat.

In a tiny wooden hut on the small jetty, the oldest man in the town sat quietly, his trousers at his knees. Then, his ablutions interrupted, he buttoned himself up and looked out, listened for a moment then sat down again, tapping his feet and smiling, and farting happily.

'Freedom loving peoples
Rise and shout
British Colonialists
All get out!'

A door in the square was thrown open and a large fat

man stood blinking in the sunlight, chest puffed, bristling with authority as he pulled on his uniform. Miguel Joubert took his job as Chief of Police seriously. His only problem was that there was never anything for him to do. Until now. Scowling officially, to hide his excitement, he marched across the square towards the radio station, his two men following him, buttoning their tunics and singing a descant to Delgado's song...

The revolutionaries were coming to the end. Garfield's fingers dancing on his keyboard, Delgado strumming his guitar, taking breath for the final sentiment.

'Throw off your chains
and follow me
I will lead you
To lib-er-teee!'

A final C chord and Delgado nodded and sat down on a stack of records. For a moment there was silence, a little motionless tableau of suspended animation, then Jay Jay tapped Delgado's shoulder.

'You through, man?'

Delgado nodded again and Jay Jay leant into the mike.

'News flash! In a daring raid earlier today, Delgado Fitzhugh seized Radio Cascara and urged the population to revolt.'

He spun his chair, picked up his binoculars and scanned the town, then turned again to the mike.

'They didn't,' he said.

A knock on the door and the Chief of Police walked in, nodded to Jay Jay, then looked at the shattered roof where the revolutionaries had smashed their way in; he took in the pile of rubble, stared at the white face of Delgado Fitzhugh, the dark eyes flashing back at him, lips compressed in righteous indignation, the Castro beard pointing defiantly at him.

In silence Miguel stepped forward, took Delgado's arm, raised him to his feet and ushered him out of the door, with Garfield following, scrawny chest puffed with pride.

11

Jay Jay watched them go before making his announcement to the island.

'He was later arrested but wanted no trouble.'

Jay Jay smiled at Eric and motioned him to come to the mike. It was almost time for the Thought For Today; but first there was money to be earned. Radio Cascara was no charity. It was a profit-making concern with shareholders to be pacified.

Again Jay Jay slid a jingle into the console and crooned over it: 'For the finest in fresh fish, go to Phil's. A fair deal for a square meal.'

The wind blasted through the window, met a squall from the hole in the roof and Jay Jay had to hang onto his hat.

The taking of the radio station was the biggest event on the island since Hurricane Alice, and a crowd of eight people had turned up at the courthouse. There would have been more. Others had intended to come but in the end apathy prevailed over curiosity as it always had.

The courthouse had not been in session for years. The old ceiling fan wasn't working and Baxter perspired heavily in his suit and tie as he read Miguel's report. He knew the story already, but Miguel would be pleased to see him reading it in front of the people; a clever man, Miguel thought, who could read without moving his lips.

It was a short report, telling how Garfield had climbed a telegraph pole on the hill above the radio station, then slid down the wire onto the roof, and how Delgado had followed him, but being heavier and less nimble, had gone straight through. The rest was history, recorded on Jay Jay's tape which lay on the bench in front of Baxter, marked Exhibit A.

The accused stood before him enjoying their moment of notoriety, wearing their berets as an act of defiance to indicate that they did not recognise the authority of the court. They had offered no defence and made no plea to the charges. They were also, as Baxter had told them, as guilty as hell.

There was a murmur in court and Baxter looked up, saw two old men at the back discussing the price of red mullet. Suppressing a yawn, he banged his gavel on the bench, startling two chickens who fluttered out of the door.

He then turned to the accused and confronted them with their fate.

'Delgado Fitzhugh and Garfield Cooper. You have heard the verdict of this court. Do you have anything to say before I pass sentence?'

Delgado turned to Garfield and gave the prearranged signal, a nod of the head. On cue, the little man began to beat out a bongo rhythm on the bench.

Do what you want
I don't give a damn
British justice
Is a farce and a sham,' sang Delgado.

Baxter battered his gavel on the bench again, narrowly missing Garfield's fingers, raising dust. Sweat pumped from Baxter's forehead, spraying the accused.

'I will not have singing in court,' he shouted with as much anger as he could muster. 'If you have something to say, it must be spoken.'

'The Rebel has vowed never to speak until it is in a free Cascara,' said Garfield.

Again Delgado nodded, then threw back his head, revealing a full set of black fillings.

'Show me no mercy
Grant me no bail
I'm ready and willing
To go to jail.'

Baxter leant across the bench and shook his head, talking to him as if he were a child.

'Delgado, I'm not sending you to jail for two reasons. One, I refuse to make a martyr of you. And two...' He glanced at his Chief of Police, 'it is still being redecorated.'

Miguel shrugged, humiliated in front of his people.

13

'Can't get the paint, boss,' he said.

Baxter sighed, gave a final bang of the gavel and the verdict was delivered. 'Six months suspended sentence...'

And Delgado scowled in disappointment.

Two

There was something about air travel, Rob Waring decided, that encouraged introspection; the lulling sense of motion perhaps, allied to the fact that on this trip he had no files to read or decisions to make, and no one waiting at the other end either to impress or be impressed by; and so he relaxed. He had been relaxing for hours now, all the way from Houston to St Thomas and now in this little helicopter throbbing south across the Caribbean.

He could feel his metabolism slowing down appreciably. He had taken his heart rate and his pulse, surreptitiously of course, in case Ben noticed and laughed. Ben was way behind him in the Spenco pecking order, but he was big enough to laugh behind Rob's back; physically big enough. Ben was a huge, red-bearded Texan and Rob felt kind of ambivalent towards him, reluctantly impressed by his strength, yet disgusted at his manners. Ben was the sort who cleaned his nails with his fork, that kind of stuff, but Rob had never mentioned it to him.

He closed his eyes and indulged himself in a little introspection. Thirty-four years old and one of the youngest middle executives in the Spenco Corporation of Houston, one of the biggest multinationals in America, which meant the *world.* He had come a long way from Poughkeepsie and had exceeded everyone's expectations of him. His parents were proud. His old High School friends were in awe of him, so much so that some of them affected to despise his status and his wealth, but he had found them out. One night, at a reunion dinner, the two snootiest, both academics, had got drunk and asked him about Andrea. They'd seen her picture in *Penthouse* and they wanted to know; and so he exaggerated, but not much and they couldn't hide the envy in their eyes...

Then there was his apartment with the uninterrupted view across the city. He could see the Spenco building from his bed. Most nights he went to sleep staring at it, measuring the gap between his office and the top floor. It wasn't far, physically speaking anyway.

He sighed and felt a twinge of fear, that familiar stab of panic that maybe he was under-achieving just a little. There were two men and a woman senior to him who were actually *younger* and that was frightening. The point was that two were from L.A. and one from New York. That was the problem of coming from Hicksville, you had to catch up. There were so many wasted years getting *metropolitan* while the young slickers were already scaling the ladder.

His nightmare was the possibility that he had already peaked. He had given himself eighteen months in which to gain promotion. If he hadn't made the thirty-ninth floor by then, he was dead. Not that he admitted any of this. He was known after all for his self-confidence. Only his shrink knew; and Andrea; and maybe Ben guessed.

'There she is, Rob!' The big man's voice startled him. He glanced at him. There was a trace of spittle on Ben's beard. Rob suppressed a shudder and followed the direction of the finger, pointing south-east.

Cascara was shrouded in cloud and all that could be seen was a stretch of shoreline. What beach there was seemed to be black but maybe it was an illusion. Rob sniffed and felt his metabolism slow still further. From here, he could see no way that Cascara was going to further his career. No way at all.

Whether it had been the unaccustomed activity of the courthouse or the sight of so many dull, obedient eyes staring at him on the way home, or a mixture of both,

Baxter did not know; but the result was that he had been galvanised into action, calling young Lucille to the house with her notepad and telling Pepito to get the files.

For the purpose of dictation he had changed back into his shorts and sweatshirt and prowled the reception room, swatting flies with a squash racket to help him concentrate.

Baxter Thwaites was the type of man who thought on his feet and sometimes Pepito found the habit distracting. A memo would start in the house and end, as surely as not, in the ganja patch.

Pepito leant against the piano surrounded by files, an ancient clipboard under his arm, waiting for his boss to come up with the correct phrases. Lucille stood by the door, pen poised over her notepad, idly kicking out at the chickens that pecked around her feet.

'Dear Minister,' Baxter said at last. 'I have still had no response to my most recent memorandum entitled: Cascara, a Plan for Economic Aid and Development. Our situation here has been grave since the banana blight of seventy-nine, which reduced production by...?' He snapped his fingers and Pepito consulted his board.

'Eighty-three per cent,' said Pepito.

Baxter nodded and continued. 'The following year our coconut crop fell...?'

'Seventy-four per cent.'

'... as a result of Hurricane Alice.' He paused. 'What little tobacco and sugar cane survived these catastrophes was subsequently devastated by the eruption of Mount Pestilence.'

At this, Lucille instinctively made the sign of the cross and curtseyed in the direction of the volcano.

'During this period,' Baxter continued, 'Britain's financial assistance to the island amounted to...?'

'Zero,' said Pepito without bothering to consult the figures.

Baxter nodded again and lashed out with his racket. 'It would seem that in the eyes of the British Government,

17

Cascara is the dot above the "i" in the word "shit".'

Pepito blinked. 'You can't say that, Governor.'

'Why not?'

'It's hardly diplomatic language,' he said sternly.

Baxter pointed at him and wagged his finger. 'That's precisely the point,' he said. 'Everything else I've sent has been filed under "Forget It". It's time to put a rocket up their arse.'

Lucille squealed and blushed at the note she had taken. Baxter apologised and she smiled at him.

'It could cost you your job, Governor,' said Pepito mournfully, thinking of his coat-tails, then looked up at the sound of a scream and saw young Estelle, the maid, being chased along the hall by Dolores. Baxter watched impassively as his wife did a lap of the room behind the girl, yelling curses in Spanish and looking for something to throw.

'My job, Pepito,' he said softly, 'is a somewhat outdated institution. Rather like my marriage.'

Pepito searched for something to say, then looked up, conscious of a growing noise from the north. The room shuddered and again Lucille crossed herself. Baxter closed his eyes, ready to welcome the liberating lava, then opened them as he recognised the sound of an engine.

He ran to the window and looked up into the belly of a helicopter heading south. The Union Jack fluttered. The two guards saluted and Baxter blinked. Two incidents in one day. Life was in danger of becoming hectic.

On the clifftop above Desolation Bay, Garfield watched his friend sitting in silence staring out to sea, towards Cuba, and felt sorry for him. If Delgado hadn't taken his vow, he would be saying that he was fed up to the back teeth. He would have said that the ball was on the slates. Three-nothing with five minutes to go. Garfield rarely understood what Delgado said, but the meaning always came through.

Garfield knew exactly what he was thinking. He would

18

be going over the books that had been washed up in the captain's trunk when the Cuban ship had gone down; the wonderful stories of Fidel and his seven men. If Fidel could take Cuba with seven, surely two was enough for Cascara.

It was bad enough having the weapons confiscated by the Governor but Delgado could live with that. What he was grieving for was the souls of his people. The place was ripe for revolution. It had a semi-literate peasant class overruled by a colonial oppressor, yet they were like sheep.

Delgado spat and Garfield sighed, thinking hard for the reason for their failure. Maybe it was historical. The books had said that the peasant classes were notoriously slow to change. What was needed was an industrial working class led by the intelligentsia, but they had no time to wait for Cascara to become industrialised. They had to make do with what they had got. It was Garfield's turn to spit over the cliff. The wind blew the spittle back into his face and he cursed. Maybe the peasants weren't worth saving. Maybe they needed something to awaken them. Maybe somebody should be shot. He glanced at Delgado, who had closed his eyes, and he wondered what the big man was planning.

Delgado was thinking of one of his father's stories, delivered through a fog of cigar smoke and whisky fumes when Delgado was just a boy. It was a story of the Highland Light Infantry on parade in Glasgow. One recruit kept getting it wrong and his mother, watching him, proudly nudged her husband and said: 'They're all out of step but our Jock.'

Maybe the old man had been right after all. It was a blasphemous thought but it wouldn't go away. He opened his eyes to find Garfield nudging him and suggesting a session of unarmed combat.

Why not? They had no weapons. They might as well get some training in. Delgado resolved to cast aside his pessimism and think positive...

19

It was Delgado who saw the helicopter first, coming over the hill behind Garfield's left shoulder. He raised both arms and nodded to Garfield to look, forgetting something he had dinned into the little man's head. Don't fall for diversionary tactics in unarmed combat. Garfield had learnt the lesson well and smartly kicked him in the balls.

It took Ben twenty minutes to inspect the rig, all sixty feet of her, and when he came back to Rob he was nodding.

'I'll get a new Kelly and a rotary table in from the Gulf,' he said, 'and we'll have this baby working in no time.'

Rob smiled and slapped him on the shoulder. The location was perfect. An old rig, disused since the fifties, perched on a clifftop, black rocks below; a wind that rattled the teeth; even the old Spenco sign on the platform was still visible after all this time. He could see that Ben thought the rust was a disgrace, but it was meant to look rough. That was the whole point of the operation. It was supposed to be a working rig producing the goods in the teeth of the elements.

He was trying to point this out when he noticed movement down the hill.

'Uh-oh,' he said. 'We are not alone.'

An odd couple, he thought, in their combat gear and berets, the white one looking like a manic Castro, walking bow-legged with a pained expression, and a small dangerous-looking black at his side.

And why the camouflage, he wondered? What could they possibly be hiding from in a dump like this?

Rob fixed his smile, the welcoming, boyish grin that had won over a hundred clients.

'Hi guys. Do you speak English?'

'I do,' said Garfield. 'My comrade will not speak until he can say: "Cascara is free".'

'Is that a political posture or a speech impediment?'

Ben grinned, then realised that Waring's question owed nothing to humour. It was a straight request for

20

information. If the young man had a sense of humour, he had strangled it at birth. A sense of humour at Spenco was a hindrance to promotion. Garfield, in turn, did not laugh.

'His posture,' he said sarcastically, 'is a promise to his people.'

'Interesting,' said Waring, then made the introductions.

'Spenco!' said Garfield, the word exploding from him. 'The ruthless Yankee capitalists?'

'Of Houston Texas,' said Rob, thinking he might as well make some use of these idiots. 'Listen,' he said, 'if we wanted to come back here, who's the person to contact?'

'Governor Thwaites,' said Garfield. 'The symbol of British oppression.'

'He sounds like our man,' Rob said, the smile still gleaming, even as the two men turned their backs on him and stalked back down the hill.

'Nice talking to you,' he shouted.

Garfield answered with a gob of spittle splattered on the rocks.

Three

For two days Dolores had been in a state of intense excitement at the prospect of entertaining the two Yankees. She had seen them from her bedroom window and for half an hour she had kept fingers and toes crossed that Baxter would invite them for dinner. Briefly she had thought of making certain by going down and personally making the invitation, but such an idea vanished as soon as it arrived. She was not made up and therefore not presentable. But Baxter, the darling, had finally done something right. They were coming at eight. Two men. At once.

She vowed to diet until then. No chocolate and only the merest sniff of tequila to calm her nerves. Once she had supervised the laying of the table, she retired to her boudoir. She chose the Balenciaga and rejected it. Maybe the backless black Chloe? She pondered for a while, gazing at her reflection, working out the angles and the percentages, and finally settled for red. She would be scarlet tonight, she thought. She would go, as the English said, the complete hog. Scarlet dress with lipstick and nails to match.

Two men. At once. She squealed and clutched herself and whimpered in anticipation ...

Eric McNab was the first to arrive, bringing with him an almost visible trough of depression. He was soaking, caught in one of Cascara's sudden squalls. Jay Jay hadn't forecast it, as usual. Indeed, Jay Jay could be malicious. Sometimes when the ganja had a hold on him, he would make up the news of hurricanes. The problem was that he wasn't wrong all the time.

The old man gratefully accepted the glass of rum from his host, despatched it in one and held his arm out for another, then slumped in an armchair, glancing at the Governor who had dressed for the occasion; a faded white dinner jacket, black trousers and bow tie. Eric tried a smile but couldn't make it. He settled himself and gazed round the room, trying to relax. He always felt at home in this room with all the booty from the wrecks, like a maritime museum; all washed up, he thought, just like himself.

He sighed and Baxter asked him what was wrong.

Eric pouted. 'You know why Delgado's doing this, don't you?'

Baxter shook his head.

'To punish his father,' said Eric.

'Why should he want to punish you?'

'For not marrying his mother,' said Eric. It was obvious, wasn't it? Surely the Governor could see that.

'Things were different in those days,' Baxter said, placing a comforting arm round the old man's shoulders, then easing himself away again as he was assaulted by rum fumes. Breath like a robber's dog, Baxter thought, but he had to try and console the old man. He looked so sad.

'Look, in those days,' he persisted, 'a Presbyterian minister couldn't marry a young island girl. Especially when he already had a wife in Edinburgh.'

Eric sighed. 'Am I never to be forgiven for one moment of weakness?'

And Baxter grinned at him. 'Our last official census showed that you've had at least fourteen moments of weakness.'

Eric nodded. It was true. It was time to beat his breast, to don sackcloth and ashes, but there were none to be found. There was only one thing for it. His left arm shot

23

out once more. It was the rum that had been his undoing. If it hadn't been for the drink, he thought ... well, he had made his bed, so he might as well lie on it.

The bell rang and a moment later Pepito ushered in the Americans. Rob had put on a Nieman Marcus Young Executive suit for the occasion, while Ben was in checked shirt and jeans, a string tie and turquoise clip, the stetson, and the Fry boots with the inch-and-a-half heels.

To Baxter they looked like a vaudeville act.

'This is most gracious of you, Governor,' said Rob.

'Not at all, old sport,' said Baxter, pouring more rum. 'We don't get many visitors here. Except for people whose ships have run aground.'

Eric nodded in agreement as the introductions were made. 'Almost the entire population of the island is descended from shipwrecked victims,' he said and Baxter winked at him, noting the 'almost'. Eric blushed, the guilt mingling with the booze, and more tiny veins popped in his cheeks.

They were in the process of toasting each other when the door was thrown open and Dolores made her entrance.

'*Bienvenido*, gentlemen,' she husked.

The four men looked at her, Rob seeing something incredibly tacky, Ben gaping at a fifteen-minute fifty-dollar hump, Eric seeing a scarlet woman who should be condemned from the pulpit, and Baxter aware once again of someone who once upon a time had been an embarrassment.

'May I present my wife.'

She tangoed into the room, holding out a hand to be kissed. Both men shook it as they introduced themselves. A smile at Rob, '*Enchanté*', and a 'Howdy' to Ben. She liked the look of Ben. Dolores had always been impressed by physical strength.

'So,' she said, fluttering the mascara at him. 'You har comm to look for oil and ...' she paused, '... seenk somm pipe.'

Baxter grinned. The years on the periphery of the

24

diplomatic world had not affected Dolores. She still talked like a hooker out of the shanties.

'No, Dolores,' he explained, speaking slowly as if to a child. 'The chaps are here to make a television commercial. Apparently our island provides a perfect setting.'

Suddenly she was interested and strove for yet more vivacity, placing her hands on her hips, striking a pose, a knee and six inches of thigh peeping through the Saint Laurent slit.

'Henny parts for me?'

Silence.

She pressed on as if auditioning. 'Do you know, at home before I marry, I was in showbizniz?'

No response. She continued like the trouper she thought she was.

'You have heard of the Great Ernesto and Dolores?'

Rob's person-to-person training obliged him to nod and Dolores' arms flew wide. The pose was now balletic, both arms above her head sending puffs of talcum from her armpits.

'I *was* Dolores.'

Baxter nodded. There was no need to respond but he could not resist it. 'I'm sure they didn't think you were Ernesto, darling.'

It was a cheap shot and Dolores treated it with the contempt it deserved. She tossed her head and stuck out her tongue at him.

The rain did not bother Delgado. It was, as his father had said, in his blood. He was a happy man again, his faith in human nature restored. Sitting in a cave at the foot of the cliffs beneath the oil rig, the waves crashing at his feet, he hummed a tune and gazed out to sea, stared at the black Cascaran sky, heavy with clouds. No stars. No moon. It was ideal. Moonlight was dangerous on a night like this when history was about to be made.

Beside him Garfield beat out a rhythm on a set of sodden bongos. They were both excited. They had waited for an hour but there was no impatience in their souls.

A blink on the horizon, the glare of a torch and Delgado whooped. Garfield got to his feet and scrabbled for his torch, answering the flash. And Delgado started singing at the top of his voice in welcome.

'Oh what a night
It's going to be
We gonna make some
His-tor-eee,
Cuban comrades
Come across the sea
Help Cascara
To lib-er-tee!'

He waved his arms in exhortation.

'Sing it louder!'

They could see the dinghy now and the outlines of two men. They seemed to be in trouble, floundering, paddles flashing, moving in circles caught in the notorious Cascaran currents.

Garfield battered the bongos and joined in Delgado's chorus.

'Help Cascara
To lib-er-tee . . .
Everybody!'

And the answering chorus came from the sea, frantic and feeble. Just one world. 'HELP.'

Garfield dropped the bongos and scurried out of the cave into the sea with Delgado behind him. As they trudged through the surf, the water pounding their thighs, Garfield was conscious that this was a historical moment. One day, when he was old, he would tell his grandchildren and the TV cameras of the night when the fledgling revolutionaries of Cascara met the might of Castro's Cuba and the torch of freedom was lit...

It took them half an hour to get the Cubans on shore and another twenty minutes before they could speak. Garfield had remembered his training, conscious of his position as Supplies Master. He had anticipated that they might be

26

uncomfortable and had brought blankets and a bottle of rum, and for twenty minutes the Cubans sat shivering, passing the bottle between them; too exhausted to be grateful, they shivered in rhythm, teeth chattering in harmony, chewing on sodden cigars.

Finally the taller one spoke, introducing himself as Angola and his friend as Jesus. No surnames. To Garfield they were almost identical with their Fidel beards and dark eyes hidden beneath the wet brims of their forage caps.

He waited with Delgado for the speech of brotherhood, and when it came he could scarcely believe his ears. Angola's accent was so thick he thought maybe he had misheard him and asked him to repeat himself.

'The answer is no,' Angola said patiently. 'Fidel says Cuba will shed blood for revolution of downtrodden people anywhere. But you people are too downtrodden even for Cuba.'

For this they had come, thought Garfield. To bring rejection? He glanced at Delgado who strummed his guitar angrily, eyes flashing. It was a dangerous moment.

'That was before
And this is now
'I'm going to change
Your mind, and how . . .'

Jesus clamped his hands over his ears and winced. 'Hold it, please,' he squealed. 'Can't you just talk to us? We nearly drowned out there.'

And Garfield had to explain again about the Rebel's vow.

'What would you be
Saying to me
If you were told
Cascara may have
A little black gold?'

And Delgado dramatically pointed to the clifftop, where the outline of the Spenco oil rig could just about be seen.

'What?' said Angola.

'*A little black gold.*'

'Oil?' said Jesus.

Garfield nodded. 'Spenco came back.'

Angola's cigar dropped onto his lap and sizzled on the blanket, then he bent over to Jesus. There was a quick muttered conference and the decision was made.

'If Spenco strike,' said Angola, 'you got yourself a deal.'

He reached into his pocket and produced two Havanas, still dry in their cases, handed them over in fraternal greeting, and for the first time since he was a child, Delgado smiled.

In Government House, the evening had followed a predictable course. Dolores was tangoing with Ben in the hall to the sound of Edmundo Ros. Eric had fallen asleep at the table, and Baxter was in expansive mood, with Pepito at his side dispensing brandy and ganja.

It was not often that he had an audience, even if the young American's bland enthusiasm was boring. But an audience was an audience.

'The first indication that this place existed comes from a ship's log in 1789,' he said. 'An Admiral named Grant discovered it, uninhabited naturally, so he ran up a flag and claimed it for the Crown. The crew picked a few mangoes and then left.'

'Fascinating,' said Rob, swallowing a yawn.

'The fact was,' Baxter continued, 'that the crew were suffering from a rather nasty occupational hazard. All that hard tack and ship's biscuits with weevils in them, and so the mangoes went down rather well. 'Course they didn't know what they were, being from Liverpool and Plaistow, but the mangoes did the trick. Within an hour a great cheer came up ...' he smiled, 'from the bowels of the ship.'

Rob nodded.

'Apparently they were still in sight of the island, so the old Admiral decided to name it Cascara.' He waited for a reaction. 'Nice, don't you think?' he prompted and again

Rob nodded, trying to conceal his bewilderment.

'After that, the French came, then the Portuguese and the Spanish but they didn't stay long. Cascara is unique, I suppose, in the history of the British Empire. No one has ever bothered to fight over it. Not a drop of blood has been spilled.'

'Really?'

'At the time this job was a big promotion for me. Youngest Governor in the Caribbean.'

At the mention of the word Caribbean, Pepito handed over a sample of the Bocachica-Bolivian Red blend. Baxter took a deep hit and offered it to Rob, an action which placed the young man in a dilemma. He had long since passed beyond the drugs phase, and he did not want Ben to see him and have anything on him, as it were. But Ben was out of the room, preoccupied with Dolores, and there was the question of hospitality to be considered. He shrugged, made his decision and nearly choked. They didn't do dope like this in Poughkeepsie.

'... over the years,' the Governor was saying, 'I think my wife has resented the restraints which the position imposes.'

On cue, Dolores swept Ben into the room and Rob hid the joint beneath the chair. The evening had not been kind to the mistress of the house. Her hair had fallen loosely but unevenly down her back. One shoulder strap had slipped and a breast was threatening to sag free. She clenched a rose between her teeth and clung to Ben as if she were drowning, one leg pushed firmly between his knees, offering a glimpse of red satin panties.

'... as you can see,' Baxter said to Rob and smiled. He made a small bow in Dolores' direction and wished her '*buenas noches*'.

She ignored him and swung Ben round and out into the hallway. Rob watched them go then turned to Baxter.

'Where did you two meet?'

'On an earlier posting of mine. I sometimes think she misses the bright lights of Guatemala City.'

Rob nodded. He missed the irony in Baxter's voice. He had never been to Guatemala City and it sounded quite exotic.

Dolores had guided Ben along the hall and into a recess under the stairs. She glanced over her shoulder to make sure that Baxter hadn't followed. Not that he would. The man had not an ounce of jealousy in him, which occasionally Dolores regretted. She had also rejected her fantasy of the two Americans at the same time. The young one was no good. From him there was no reaction, and so Dolores jumped to the obvious conclusion. Rob Waring must be *maricon*.

But Ben was certainly a hundred per cent male. There was no doubt about it. She pushed herself even closer into him and Ben didn't complain. He was still wearing his stetson and his boots, and when he spoke his voice was surprisingly high-pitched. Excitement had always affected his vocal chords.

'Anytime you're in Port Arthur, Texas, you look me up, Dolores. We'll split a fifth of Wild Turkey, feed Waylon into the juke box and boogie till we puke.'

'Port Arthur, Texas,' Dolores murmured. 'Eet sounds wonderful. He promised me Paris, Rome, Washington ... and he geeves me the peets.'

And with that she reached for his hat, pulled down his head and thrust her tongue down his throat.

Four

The Cascara file in the Foreign Office library was too slim to have attracted much dust, but what there was got up Sarah Treadwell's nose as she took it from the shelf. Her nostrils quivered for a moment as she fought a sneeze. It wouldn't do to sneeze in front of the clerks; wouldn't be at all dignified.

Sarah did not go directly to her desk. Instead she locked herself in the loo and flipped through the file. It wasn't that she was in any way interested in Cascara, not *intrinsically*, as one of the Nigels would have said. It was simply that she wanted to appear well-informed in front of Sir Malcolm.

She had been secretary to Sir Malcolm Leveridge of the Foreign and Commonwealth Office for almost a year now, and was ever so slightly pissed-off that he had made no attempt to *bonk* her. She was attractive enough, for goodness sake, and so it was about time. She read the file, yawned and checked her appearance. Sarah was five feet ten of County stock and one day would marry one of the Nigels. She hadn't yet decided which. Meanwhile there was the question of Sir Malcolm. He was not what any of her friends would consider obvious material, being almost fifty and rather staid, but on the credit side he was said to be very fit; the squash champion at his club, so it was rumoured, and what was more, he was well in with the Foreign Secretary, which meant he was well in with most of the Cabinet, which meant that he actually knew *Michael*, who was very much bonking material.

Slowly she composed herself and made her way to her desk, knocked on Sir Malcolm's door and handed him the file, glanced at the picture of Lady Leveridge on his desk, a dull-eyed woman with two chins dissected by a string of pearls, then left with Sir Malcolm's thank-you-my-dear wafting behind her.

Three hours later Sir Malcolm had finally cornered the Foreign Secretary. The old man had been putting him off for days, saying that he was tied up, but finally he'd consented to a ten-minute audience in St James's Park.

It was a dull day and drizzling. They shared a brolly and walked quickly, bowlers almost touching, the old man's hands deep in his pockets.

'Sorry to drag you away from lunch, Minister,' said Sir Malcolm. He hadn't dragged him away but the old man was known to be fond of people who apologised.

'Not at all, Malcolm. We don't see enough of each other. How's Margaret?'

'Marjory.'

'Splendid woman, your wife. And the boys? Still at school are they?'

'The girls have just left school. They're at secretarial colleges.' It was all a bit tedious, this forgetfulness, but at least it wasn't devious, like some of them in the House who actually pretended not to know your damned wife's name.

'Well,' said the old man. 'I've enjoyed our chat.'

And he was off, taking his brolly with him, and Sir Malcolm had to run to catch up.

'I did want to have a confidential word about Cascara,' he said.

The old man twitched, startled as if he had just been wakened by the division bell.

'Cascara,' he said, with a gruesome smile which was well known in the House to convey bafflement. 'Remind me. Who does that belong to?'

'Us.'

'Us? Yes, of course. Us. And the situation is as volatile as ever in the ... ah ...'

'Caribbean.'

'Quite.'

Sir Malcolm lowered his voice and glanced around him. You never knew who was listening these days; bugs in the rose bushes and all that. Maybe it was paranoia but, what with Bulgarians being stabbed by poisoned brollies and Libyans running riot, there was no telling. Quietly he delivered the message.

'The CIA have informed us that there's a danger of the Cubans landing on Cascara, running up their flag and giving us another Falklands situation.'

'Wonderful,' said the old man, beaming in the drizzle. 'Maggie would love it.'

Sir Malcolm shook his head and tried to explain. 'The Falklands cost a fortune. And once the dust had settled, it was pretty hard to justify the expense of defending British lives, most of whom were sheep.'

The old man shrugged and asked what the alternative was.

Sir Malcolm lowered his voice still further. 'Pull the plug on the place now,' he said. 'Wrap it up, lock stock and barrel.'

The Foreign Secretary shook his head. He was one of the old school and had never really become accustomed to the idea of giving the Empire back. He remembered the globe being boldly painted red. He would have preferred the old days when they were building the Empire and fooling the natives.

He tried to protest, knowing that he was at a disadvantage. He talked about Hong Kong and Gibraltar but Leveridge didn't seem impressed. Dammit, he'd done his homework. He even knew where the bloody place was. He groped in his brain for a plan and found one.

'If it's in the Caribbean,' he said, 'surely we could encourage tourism?'

'No beach,' said Sir Malcolm.

'No beach?' he repeated dumbly.

'And apparently there's a dreadful wind which blows in all directions at once.'

The old man was finally convinced. 'Must make a hand of bridge rather difficult,' he said.

'Almost impossible, I imagine.'

And that was that. If there was another solution, then the Foreign Secretary, caught cold in the middle of the park, couldn't think of it.

'Very well,' he said. 'Do as you see fit, Malcolm. As long as the people don't end up here driving our buses.'

'We'll make alternative arrangements for the population, Minister,' said Sir Malcolm.

'Jolly good.'

The old man wandered off. There had been precedents after all. When they couldn't give the island of Aldabra in the Indian Ocean away to the Americans because of the fuss from conservationists about giant tortoises, they had simply moved the people off Diego Garcia to Mauritius. And hardly anyone noticed.

He waddled back to the House, muttering about having lunch some time and would Sir Malcolm give his love to Marigold.

'Silly old sod,' said Sir Malcolm, but softly, so that neither the Minister nor the bugs could hear.

He almost ran back to the office.

'He bought it,' he said to Sarah. 'He's passing on my recommendation to the Prime Minister.'

Sarah beamed. 'Gosh, super, Sir Malcolm. Congrats. It's so rare these days that people in power have the courage to make tough decisions.'

Sir Malcolm beamed back at her. His name would be brought to the attention of the PM at last. Sarah was looking at him with what he thought was admiration, like a well-bred puppy. Idly he wondered if she would like her tummy rubbed.

Five

The Governor was enjoying a game of cricket on the lawn with a few chaps from the port, and in his fantasy he was wreaking vengeance on the West Indies for their destruction of the England Test side. At Millfield he was considered something of a batsman. His position was number three, the hardest in the game, the slot no one wanted. He was Graveney that morning, about to sweep some six-feet-six bowler from Tobago over the Oval gasometer, when Pepito spoiled it all by running across the wicket and putting the eleven-year-old bowler off his run.

Pepito was excitedly waving a piece of pink paper, the colour of which Baxter vaguely remembered. It was a telegram; an *incoming* telegram, and Pepito's accent had changed gear with excitement and had become more Eton than Eton.

London had answered the rocket up the arse.

Baxter read it, grinned, and ran up the hill to the house and spotted Dolores sitting on the porch. She was naked beneath a housecoat, one foot on the rail, tongue out, concentrating on painting her toenails. To her left Nado stood with a silver tray and a martini shaker, ignoring her nakedness. He had seen it all before and was not impressed. She, for her part, ignored him, just to show who was boss around here.

Baxter panted up to her and called her name. She did not look up.

'I am beezee, Baxter. I am watching my nails dry.'

'I have some exciting news,' he said, and she was suddenly interested, in the expectation of celebration.

'We are leaving? There ees a God?'

'No. Sir Malcolm Leveridge is coming here on an official visit from London. My rocket has brought results.'

Dolores shrugged. If it was not an exodus, at least it was something different, but there was just one patently obvious problem which her husband had failed to anticipate.

'I heff nothink to werr,' she said, but Baxter had already gone, thinking of preparations, of bunting and brass bands and of lording it over some whey-faced pipsqueak from Whitehall; of putting Cascara on the map.

Jay Jay was having a good time. For once he had real news to broadcast, and so he told his listeners on the hour and the half hour that Her Majesty's representative was coming to visit in two days' time and they had to put their best faces forward.

The island's only entrepreneur was also a happy man. Ah Fong had been the sole survivor of a ship that went down in Hurricane Alice and was the first and only Chinese Cascaran. He had been quick to open up a business and had soon begun to thrive because there was no competition; now the whole population was at his door taking advantage of the Governor's offer of free paint to freshen up the town for the visit, the bill to be picked up by Her Majesty's Government. Everyone had taken advantage and by noon a heat haze of gloss and emulsion had risen over the port and the place throbbed to the sound of coughing and spluttering.

Even Garfield had joined the queue ordering Ah Fong's complete stock of aerosol sprays.

At Government House the flag-pole was being painted, the flag ironed and a coat of whitewash slapped on the front of the house. In the reception room Dolores spat on the portrait of the Queen and wiped it clean, determined that the glass should shine until she could see her face in it.

The two policemen were dragging one of the cannons up the hill to the headland, following the Governor's orders to have it ready to fire a salute. No one knew where the cannons had come from but there were many stories. They were identical and without any markings, just five feet of rusted iron with two balls at the base, symbols for generations of island girls who stroked the barrels and giggled into their hands.

There had been a brief problem. Where to get the gunpowder? Then one of the policemen had a brainwave, dug out Delgado's confiscated bandoleer and emptied the bullets.

In the garage Pepito had kicked a brooding hen and a cat with a litter of kittens out of the old Daimler and was trying to restore it to its former glory, while Baxter was getting over a nasty moment. Someone had ordered two young men to tidy up the garden, and he had stopped them and their machetes just as they reached the Bocachica. Having averted that crisis, he decided to go down to the port to see what was happening. He hopped onto his bike and pedalled down the hill, waving to a couple of men who were painting over Delgado's anti-British slogans.

When he reached the square he whistled in amazement. He had never seen the place so busy. Everyone had a job to do. Miguel was conducting the town band. He had dug out a few battered brass instruments to go with the steel drums. Baxter wondered what they were trying to play. There was a vague hint of 'Rule Britannia' to a funji rhythm. 'Needs work,' he told Miguel and cycled off to the pier, where Martha, the schoolteacher, was vainly trying to organise her pupils into some kind of order.

Martha was slim and pretty, not yet a victim to the ravages of rum and multiple childbirth, and innocent enough to blush when Baxter asked her what she was doing. The kids stopped fighting for a moment as he stared at them, each one wearing an aviator cap, courtesy of a sunken troopship, with a placard attached on which was painted a single letter.

'It's my idea, Governor,' she said. 'When Sir Malcolm arrives, he'll see their little heads spelling out a message of welcome.'

So sweet, he thought. She was so much sweeter than her kids who grumbled and fought among themselves. He patted her arm and told her to be careful; better not have any Fs or Ks in the message. They didn't want anything rude to greet Her Majesty's representative.

Martha blushed as she watched him pedal away, thinking that maybe the Governor wasn't such an educated man after all and that perhaps English public schools were overrated, for surely there were no Fs or Ks in 'Welcome Sir Malcolm'; but she made a mental note to check her dictionary, just in case.

Only the Reverend McNab was in any kind of trouble. Her name was Millicent, a seventeen-year-old Creole, and she was resisting his idea that she should leave town for a couple of days until the visit was over. She had tried to sway him with tears, then anger, and finally sex, but he withstood everything, even the groping of her little, well-practised hand. The old man was proud of himself, that finally he had overcome the temptations of the flesh, although it was made easier for him by the fact that Millicent was seven months pregnant and he had always been turned off by bulk.

Finally she bowed to reason and a five-pound note. As she climbed the hill, clutching a battered suitcase, she saw Delgado and waved at him. He was standing beside a newly-painted wall waiting for it to dry so that he could get busy with his aerosol. Silently Delgado saluted her and puffed a spray of black paint in the air in greeting.

With the arrival of Deke Halliday on Cascara, Rob Waring had a problem. Everything had gone fine until then. The crew was happy with the accommodation in the trailers in the compound and Sam Crespi, the director, had been the soul of charm, not the least bit stand-offish as one might expect of one of the country's great directors of commercials with three Emmys to his credit – one of them for Pepsi – and a feature for Warners upcoming.

Sam was okay. Then Deke arrived and immediately there was tension. Deke was late, but that was to be expected. When you've been a big star, you're late on purpose, almost by instinct. In the old days, when he was on the up, Deke was known for his professionalism. Sometimes he would turn up on set early to give himself a good name vis-a-vis the prima donnas; but that was when he was nudging real fame, when he was above the title.

Now he was too old. Earlier that year he had suffered the worst indignity of his entire career. His agent had rung and told him he was being considered for a cameo role as Nastassia Kinski's father, and he broke down. Who the hell wanted to play Kinski's *father*, for God's sake? Plus, he didn't even get the part.

That night he had broken down in the Polo Lounge and admitted that he was too old for Kinski, and now everyone despised him. He thought only his analyst knew about his Kinski fantasies but now he had admitted them. Twice. On consecutive nights, and what was worse, he was so wrapped up in his personal tragedy and had so much bourbon in him that he did not even remember his confessions.

He did not even notice the sneers and the laughter behind their hands. His antennae, so reliable when young, were now as limp as his dick, or so one of his erstwhile fans had whispered; nor was he aware of a remark, made by an English writer, that plastic surgery had helped take ten years off him and bourbon had put most of them back.

And so now he was tense. He did not want to come to Cascara to make this crummy commercial. He wanted to be Richard Gere.

Now they were an hour behind schedule because Deke wouldn't come out of his trailer, because his trailer wasn't quite as big as Crespi's. The crew were becoming

39

impatient. The light was fading and finally Rob persuaded Crespi to go and see him. Muttering: 'The mountain goes to Mahomet', Crespi obliged. Ten minutes later he came out.

'What's the problem?' Rob asked.

'He's not happy.'

'Not happy?' Rob squeaked. 'He's making a quarter of a million dollars to recite a commercial off cue cards, and he's not happy?'

'You gotta remember he was a big star, Rob,' said Crespi. 'And stars need stroking. They need masseurs and limos and fruit in the bathroom.'

Rob shook his head. Stroking indeed. He searched the sky for inspiration and found none. It was his job to get the work done on time and within budget, so if he had to stroke Deke Halliday, then he had better get on with it. As he was psyching himself up for the ordeal, the trailer door opened and Deke emerged, wearing a red boiler suit designed by Bill Blass and a petulant expression.

As he reached them, he automatically turned to his left and offered his profile, the jaw that once was lantern, the features that once were matinee.

'Is it too much to ask for some ice?'

Rob held up his hands in mock surrender and wheedled. 'Deke, I'm sorry, but Cascara's pretty short on amenities. I mean, that's why we're here. Spenco has to convince the public that it will go any place, suffer any discomfort, to ease the energy crisis.'

Sam nodded in agreement. 'Hell-holes of the world. That's the campaign, Deke.'

Deke, under attack from two fronts, turned to face them, hands on hips.

'Yeah, but do we have to *go* to the hell-holes of the world? Couldn't we shoot in Burbank with back projection? Shit, I made "Night Train To Rangoon" without leaving the lot. Not to mention "The Last Voyage of Sinbad".'

Rob reached for his arm and Deke backed away. 'People

want grainy reality these days, Deke,' he said.

'My agent never mentioned grainy reality.'

Rob reached him, put an arm round his shoulder in the hope that Deke was beginning to come round. There had been something in the way he mentioned his agent that suggested he was beginning to co-operate, just a touch of petulance which Rob took to mean a final spasm of dignity in the face of a lost cause.

'Later I'll get you everything you need,' he whispered. 'Ice. Soap...'

'I want a woman.'

And Rob knew he had won. 'You got it,' he said. 'And how about some grass? They smoke lethal weed round here.'

Deke brightened. 'Better make it two women.'

They went to work.

An hour later they still hadn't got it right.

'Hell-holes of the world,' yelled the clapper boy. 'Slate one, take eleven.'

Sam yelled for the drill to be activated and pointed to his star... 'And go, Deke.'

Deke stepped into shot, and smiled.

'Hi,' he said. 'I'm Deke Halliday for Spenco. As I see it, we Americans have two choices. Sure, we can let OPEC put the screws on till our eyes water. Or we can do it the American way. Quit beefing. Get off our butts and go find the oil for ourselves. That's why me and the guys are here on Cascara.' He smiled, shook his head and counted a beat.

'No, your travel agent won't have heard of it. But we're not here for a picnic. We're here on this forbidding, God-forsaken, windswept island to show...'

At that point the wind shifted, a squall hit the cliff and took off with Deke's toupee, the actor's scream harmonising with his director's yell to 'Cut, Cut, for Chrissakes, Cut...'

It took Rob another forty minutes to coax Deke back out of the trailer and throughout the ordeal he was thinking there should be professional people for this, professional masseurs of the ego, salaried. He shouldn't have to do all this. This wasn't what he joined Spenco for. Hell, he never even liked Deke Halliday when the man was half-famous.

Finally the star reckoned that he had sulked enough. He had checked the light. It was time to come out. He didn't want to have to spend another day on this damned piece of rock.

He emerged once more, smiled at the make-up girl and sat down on a canvas chair. She smiled back at him as she fixed his face and diplomatically rubbed a breast against his shoulder, which seemed to help, then eased a hard hat onto his head.

Deke winced. 'I don't feel comfortable in this hat.'

And now it was Sam's turn. 'Deke, just try it this way,' he wheedled. 'Then we have a choice. At least we keep shooting till we find the toup.'

Deke pouted into the mirror. 'But why a yellow hat? Yellow's such a faggy colour.'

'We're not shooting a shampoo commercial,' said Sam, who was rapidly running out of patience.

Deke snapped his fingers at the props girl and threw her the hat. 'Get me one in plaid,' he said. Sam grunted an oath and was about to lose his temper when he was interrupted by the sound of an engine.

He turned to see a Land Rover draw up by the gate and a big man dressed in khaki get out, followed by some kind of dago broad in a pencil skirt, high heels and a ridiculous hat. Again he swore and sank into his seat, thinking that Spielberg never had such problems.

Baxter was halfway through the gate when he was stopped by a squeal of protest from his wife.

'I cannot walk on thees,' she said, tapping her toe at the mud. 'I will ruin my best shoes.'

Baxter turned and looked at her. 'I told you to wear boots,' he said, his mind flashing up a memory of childhood, of playing in a puddle in his sandals and his mother spanking him.

'How can I meet a film star in boots,' she complained. 'You must carry me.'

Baxter flared his nostrils and snorted as he had been taught in school.

'You can't be serious, Dolores,' he said.

She folded under the attack. The combination of supercilious Englishman and Cascaran mud had defeated her. She knew only how to attack, to scream and throw t ings, but she was stuck in the mud and helpless.

'Where has all the magic gone?' she said softly.

'I didn't realise you wanted magic,' he said, his voice corrupt with sarcasm. 'When we get home, I'll lay you on the table and saw you in half.'

Baxter snickered, then turned as Rob came towards him, hand outstretched in welcome, saying what-a-pleasant-surprise.

'We're having this state visit tomorrow,' said Baxter, 'so we wondered if you and Mister Halliday could attend the official lunch.'

Rob smiled in delight, then frowned. Deke might not have got his words right by then and they were already over budget. 'Very kind,' he said, but I don't know what Deke has planned.'

'Meester Halliday,' said Dolores, tiptoeing past him, clutching her hat, 'Wherr is he? Is that him over there?'

She stumbled off in the direction of the set. Watching her, Baxter wondered what had happened to the rose between her teeth. Probably been excreted by the Texan, he thought.

Deke got off his chair as he saw her and nudged Sam. 'Hey,' he said. 'You guys finally got your ass in gear. Now all we need is the ice and two glasses.'

'Meester Halliday,' Dolores said as she reached them. 'Thees, for me, is a great pleasure.'

'For both of us, I hope, baby,' he said.

She held out her hand thinking of 'Night Train'. This time, for sure, her hand would be kissed. Surely.

It wasn't. Deke grabbed her, pulled her into an embrace,

43

puffed halitosis into her face and groped her bottom with both hands. Dolores blinked, then stumbled back as Rob rushed up and forced them apart.

'Deke,' he said, the grin in place. 'Have you met Mrs Thwaites?'

'Later, Waring,' said Deke hungrily, grabbing at her again. 'We'll be in my trailer.'

He caught her flailing arm and began to drag her through the mud.

'This,' said Rob, 'is the Governor's wife.'

The word 'Governor' did not faze Deke. Nor the word 'wife'. He'd had many a wife in his time, Governor's or not. But the message was clear enough. He had been let down, in this hell-hole.

'You mean,' he roared as if playing Lear, 'this is not the hooker?'

Dolores was enraged. She turned and glared at her husband.

'Baxter, did you hear this?' This was a slight to her honour. This was a duel at dawn. This was castration.

'I told you not to wear those shoes,' said Baxter.

Briefly there was a stand-off, Dolores horrified, Deke sulking, Rob confused, Baxter quietly amused, then the tableau was broken by a belch from the bowels of the earth and a shudder as the rig began to vibrate.

The oil men were the first to react, dropping to their knees, ears to the ground, the others turning to stare at one another in apprehension, Baxter recalling the war, Dolores an earthquake in Guatemala, Deke the applause at the Academy Awards on the night he had almost been nominated...

'Jesus, it's a strike,' said Rob.

'It can't be,' said Baxter. 'Surely?' But he wasn't convinced.

As they watched, Ben ran up and roared into Rob's face the one phrase that meant more to an oil man than beer, women or Waylon Jennings.

'*She's gonna blow!*'

Even as the last spray of spittle hit Waring in the face, the cap exploded and the gusher roared forty feet high. Then it dropped for a moment and spurted again, higher this time, drenching them in a clear, warm liquid.

Sam gazed at it with a director's eye, cursing his ill-luck that the cameras weren't rolling.

'What is it?' he yelled, trying to make himself heard.

'It sure ain't oil,' said Ben.

'Jesus Christ,' said Deke, holding onto his hat. 'I gave up a "Love Boat" to do this.'

All Dolores knew was that she was being soaked to the skin. Her favourite Chloe was ruined and that foul-mouthed ham actor was trying to drag her into his trailer. She kicked backwards, connected with something soft, heard him gasp and tottered off towards the Land Rover. She hadn't been so miserable since her wedding night and she permitted herself the luxury of tears, for no one would notice in all this rain.

Meanwhile Ben was shaking his head, caught between tears and laughter, aware of the absurdity of the situation.

'Can you believe it?' he said. 'Spenco strikes water.'

Rob had been holding his hardhat when the gusher gushed and now it was filling with water. Without thinking he stuck his finger in and tasted it.

'It's not regular water,' he said. 'It has...' he searched for the phrase, '... natural effervescence.'

He passed his hat to Baxter who tasted it and nodded approvingly.

'With a kind of tangy, lemony flavour.'

Rob was the first to react. At that moment he realised why he was made of executive material. It was all to do with foresight and quick reactions. He grabbed Ben's arm and pulled him a few yards to one side, away from prying ears.

And when he spoke his voice was staccato and authoritative.

'I want this site sealed. I want this fence fixed and I

want signed affidavits from all personnel that if they breathe a word of this, we'll have their ass.'

'Why, for Chrissake?' said Ben.

'Because,' Rob whispered, 'we've struck friggin' Perrier.'

Six

The great day arrived, hot and windy, and long before noon Baxter was feeling the strain. Either he had put on weight or the ceremonial white uniform had shrunk; or maybe Dolores, in one of her more bizarre fantasies, had been trying it on. The sword was uncomfortable, the hat felt silly and there were soup stains on the collar, but it would have to do. He left the bedroom and made his way downstairs, hearing as ever the discordant screech of his wife and the roosters.

Dolores was once again in a state of excitement, dressed in black and raging at Nado. The problem, it seemed, was the napkins. To Baxter the table looked perfect. He knew that Nado had spent hours laying it and he could see the pride on the young face. Each piece of cutlery was equidistant from its neighbour. The glasses were at the correct angle of forty-five degrees north-east of the placemats but Dolores had spotted a blunder.

'Paper napkins,' she screeched. 'For a state dinner?'

She was a gruesome sight with her rollers in her hair and a Margarita in her fist.

'I'll get the linen, ma'am,' said Nado humbly.

Baxter moved between them and Dolores wrinkled her nose. 'You smell of mothballs.'

'And you smell of tequila, dearest. But I'm more concerned with why you've changed these place settings.'

'Because I weesh to seet next to Sir Malcolm.'

'But that means that Eric will sit next to our beauty queen.' He spread his arms in exasperation and glared at

47

her, cursing her stupidity. 'How can we maintain the dignity of the occasion when our spiritual leader is trying to get his hand up Miss Cascara's skirt?'

'You prefer his hand up *my* skirt,' she challenged him.

'At least you're accustomed to it. You won't scream.'

With that, Baxter spun on one heel and left the room, with Nado calling after him that he would change the seating arrangements.

Dolores stared at her husband's back, anger boiling in her. She couldn't get at him and so she turned to the nearest victim, grabbed the tablecloth and began to walk out.

'Oh, and Nado...' she said, grimacing at him as the first knife and fork tinkled onto the tiles followed by a wine glass. As she reached the door, the rest followed behind her, a glorious cacophony of crashing, smashing, tinkling and banging... 'I said the *lace* tablecloth.'

Nado stared at the culinary carnage and then at his mistress as she marched down the hall, thinking of all the various ways he would dispose of her body. Nado was proud of his pure negroid blood. There had been no dilution since the old slave days, and he thought of Hispanics as inferior. It was to his eternal shame that he was forced to work for this slag from Guatemala. One day, though, he promised himself that he would have his revenge; and it would be sweet.

As he began to clear up the mess, he was aware of the lurching presence of the Reverend McNab. He looked up to see the old man dressed in his best Presbyterian grey, the sombre outfit highlighting his red cheeks.

'Where's the Governor?' Eric asked.

Nado pointed down the hall and Eric turned to see Baxter walking towards him, looking eight feet tall in his white suit and plumed hat.

Eric had always been impressed by ceremony and ritual, and secretly wished that he had been born a Catholic so that he could dress up. When he spoke, the awe was genuine.

48

'You look splendid, Baxter.'

'I feel as if I'm wearing a live chicken on my head,' said the Governor.

Jay Jay felt as if he had been temporarily castrated, if such a thing were possible. For the first time since he had opened the radio station, he had been forbidden to broadcast; on the Governor's orders. He had promised not to sabotage the great day with a blast of the Wailers, but the Governor did not trust him and had taken away his transformer, just in case.

For half an hour or so Jay Jay felt aggrieved and even thought of throwing in his lot with Delgado, but then he had worked out the consequences. He'd heard Radio Cuba: all those messages exhorting the people to work, the endless outpourings from Tass, the continual martial music, hours of boredom and no back-beat; and so he swallowed his pride and gave himself the day off, but he did not move from his post. He resolved to sit and watch the proceedings through his binoculars and make a mental tape of the event, just like Walter Cronkite and that Englishman who did Lady Di's wedding, whatever his name was.

He scanned the square, taking in the whole population of the island, dressed as if for church, Ah Fong moving among them selling Union Jacks, the Missus Governor on a reviewing stand in the middle of the square, smiling and waving with a circular motion of the hand, elbow fixed. No one was taking any notice of her.

He saw the Governor and Pepito down by the quay and a bunch of kids with letters on their heads, and Miguel's steel band polishing their instruments.

Then he swung the binoculars out to sea and became the first Cascaran to catch sight of the British naval cutter as it came into view around the headland. First he focused on the pennants, then down the mast to the man in pin-stripes and bowler hat, and the red leather briefcase.

'Here come de man,' said Jay Jay, sighing happily, coveting the bowler. What a hat for the dreadlocks, he thought, and wondered where he could get hold of one.

Briefly he was stabbed with a pang of regret that he could not tell this story as it happened and he glanced at his useless microphone, then shrugged and focused on Sir Malcolm's face. He had never seen such a white face with its strange lopsided sneer. Then the man was turning to look at something and Jay Jay followed his gaze and saw Mrs Whitehall coming out of the cabin.

Jay Jay whistled in approval. This was the white ass of his fantasies. Six feet of it, maybe, in an off-the-shoulder dress and sun hat, alabaster skin like he had read about in Barbara Cartland but never seen in the flesh. She came up to Sir Whitehall and together they stood at the rail looking towards the volcano, Sir Whitehall stroking Lady Whitehall's bottom.

'Ah, that's nice,' said Jay Jay, wishing that he could tell the island that all was well with the great man's marriage...

Sarah's first glimpse of Cascara made her slightly apprehensive.

'I must say the coast looks frightfully dangerous,' she observed.

'My dear,' said Sir Malcolm, 'throughout its history, Cascara has only ever been a navigational hazard.'

She nodded and sighed. It wasn't quite what she expected and said so. 'I only wish my first trip to the Caribbean had been to somewhere more romantic.'

Sir Malcolm's hand patted her bottom. 'Once my painful duty is behind me,' he said, 'I thought I'd show you the delights of St Lucia for a few days.'

And Sarah beamed.

Sir Malcolm gripped the rail as the cutter swept into the harbour. A most peculiar sight greeted them and Sir Malcolm groaned deep into his waistcoat. It was like something out of an old Movietone newsreel, only in colour. As they got closer, he could make out a group of children lined up with a message on their heads:

MELCOLM
SIR WALCOME

'Christ,' he said. It was ... he searched for the phrase ... a time warp; the crumbling jetty, the strip of black sand; and the people! Motley, that was the word, ranging from blue-black to albino with what looked like a group of six-foot Scandinavians among them. He blinked. That must be what's-his-name?-Thwaites by the quay, looking like something out of Madame Tussaud's, with some black chappie by his side and damn me, he thought, if the black isn't offering him a ciggie and the chap is taking it, a quick puff, then handing it back again and the black chappie hiding it behind his back.

And then the engines were cut and they were coasting in and, would you believe it, some native kids were leaping into the sea around them and swimming like dolphins, probably asking for coins. Ye Gods, he muttered, what next?

The cutter bumped against the quay and he clambered out, whispering to Sarah that he wouldn't be long. As he moved forward there was a terrific explosion from the headland. He stopped, startled, and looked up at a cloud of smoke and what appeared to be shrapnel flying around, then Thwaites was in front of him, pulling the sword from his scabbard and waving it about so that he was forced to duck. Then he held out his hand in welcome and Sir Malcolm shook it and the crowd was cheering, so that his words of welcome were drowned and Sir Malcolm had to lip-read.

As they made their way along the jetty, Sir Malcolm grunted, not bothering to conceal his irritation.

'What's all this, Thwaites? I cabled you to say I was coming over for a quiet word in your ear and you've laid on a bloody carnival.'

Baxter smiled at him. 'The people are rather excited, sir. This is their first official visit since 1898.'

51

They reached the end of the jetty and the band struck out with something resembling the National Anthem and Sir Malcolm instantly stood to attention. He wanted to check his watch. There wasn't a lot of time, but he had to wait till they had finished. The Queen, after all, was the Queen.

Then it was over. Good, he thought and made to move, but the band had stopped for only the briefest moment before launching into some dirge or other. He glanced at Thwaites and saw him making strange arm movements, as though he were swimming, and all the other idiots were doing the same. As he stood there, he was nudged in the ribs and Thwaites was nodding to him to follow suit.

'The Cascaran Anthem, sir,' he explained.

Cursing beneath his breath, Sir Malcolm did as he was asked.

'What are they all doing?' he asked.

'The breaststroke,' said Baxter. 'You see, they're all descended from shipwreck victims.'

Then the Governor was singing with the others and nudging Sir Malcolm to follow the chorus.

'Lord help your servants
In the sea
Please take time
To rescue me
In the distance
Can it be
Glory Glory
Cascara tree.'

Sir Malcolm felt the sweat drip down his arms. He had never known anything so ridiculous. He hadn't got where he was today by doing the bloody breaststroke on a bloody quayside; but at last it was over, a final blast of the trumpets, followed by merciful silence.

Again Sir Malcolm stepped forward only to be restrained by Pepito. He gazed at Thwaites and the crowd. Now they were all leaning back, gazing at the sky, arms windmilling backwards. And the band was playing again.

> *'Thank you Father*
> *For this land*
> *It is bountiful*
> *And grand*
> *We will stay*
> *Your faithful band*
> *Praying rescue's*
> *Near at hand.'*

Diplomacy was everything, and so Sir Malcolm finished the backstroke with the others until it was over. Dizzy with exertion, half-blind from staring at the sun, he clutched his briefcase and swayed, watching the mad Governor giving three 'hips' and the crowd responding with 'hoorays'. It was indeed a time warp. No question, and now he was being led to an ancient Daimler coupé like something out of a gangster movie, was vaguely aware of a black hand helping him in and of being asked by the Governor to stand in the back, the better to acknowledge the cheers of the crowd. Then the driver found the wrong gear, reversing the damn thing so that they were pitched forward, a scream from someone in the front as the Governor's sword stuck him in the shoulder, then they were thrown back again into the upholstery, knees in the air.

He had never felt such embarrassment in all his career, with Sarah watching too, but it had its compensations. He was going to enjoy the next few minutes.

He glanced at the crowd, dull eyes staring back at him, Union Jacks waving, flowers being thrown at him, two police outriders on bicycles flanking him unsteadily.

Baxter wiped the blood from his sword, checked that Pepito was okay, then turned and beamed at his guest.

'Do you wish to address the nation, Sir Malcolm?'

'Certainly not,' he replied. 'Drive on.'

The car was approaching a dangerous-looking piece of carpentry which Sir Malcolm took to be a reviewing stand. On it stood some dreadfully overdressed dago floozie smiling at him. He leant forward and groaned, and tapped the driver on the shoulder.

'Get a move on, will you,' he said. 'Thanks to this shindig, I'm already five minutes behind schedule. I'm lunching aboard HMS *Hermes* at one.'

He caught a quick flash of disappointment on the floozie's face, barely concealed by the mask of make-up, as the car swept past the reviewing stand and turned to make a lap of the square, then Thwaites was looking at him, baffled like a puppy that's been unexpectedly kicked.

'But we've arranged lunch here, followed by a cricket match, and then we have to discuss Cascara's future.'

Sir Malcolm shook his head and slowly explained the real world to this buffoon.

'The point of my visit, Thwaites, is to inform you that Cascara has no future.'

'What?'

In reply Sir Malcolm handed him a leather-bound memo from his briefcase. Baxter opened it and stared at one piece of paper, and had to read it twice to understand.

He was so preoccupied that he did not see Delgado and Garfield sprint from the crowd and throw themselves to the ground in the classic prone position of civil disobedience; but they had not chosen their ground well. They lay on their backs at one of Port Agnes' few T-junctions. The Daimler simply turned right, spraying them with dust.

By the time the memo had sunk into Baxter's brain, the car was already back at the jetty and Sir Malcolm was getting out. Baxter leapt out after him, anger beginning to build in him, an emotion he had long thought submerged beneath clouds of ganja. He caught up with him, grabbed an arm, spun him round and spluttered at him.

'You can't close down an island like a bankrupt business. What about the people? Are you going to offer them independence?'

Sir Malcolm pulled his arm free, affronted by the physical assault.

'Certainly not,' he snapped. 'We'll relocate them on one of our other islands – St Michael, a much more agreeable place, and it has a beach. We're putting in an airstrip, a couple of hotels and a nine-hole golf course. So we'll be needing labourers and ultimately a lot of waiters.'

He turned and stepped into the cutter, leaving Baxter stranded.

'And what are they being offered in compensation?' he shouted over the noise of the engines. 'A stipend? A bag of seed and a mud hut?'

'I'm not sure we'll go that far,' said Sir Malcolm.

Then he had disappeared into the cabin with not even a wave of the hand, only the cutter making waves as it made a tight circle and headed west.

Baxter raged impotently, suddenly conscious of the weight of the ridiculous hat which had become in that moment a symbol of betrayal. With a roar he swept it off and flung it into the sea, where it bobbed in the wake of the cutter, no longer a live chicken, more a dying swan.

He turned and strode along the jetty to the square, trying to think how he was going to tell the people, avoiding their trusting eyes.

At the reviewing stand he walked past Dolores, ignoring her questions, tapped the mike and held up his hands for silence.

A crowd of Union Jacks fluttered at him.

'Citizens,' he said. 'Friends, I don't quite know how to tell you this, but I have grave news.'

The flags still waved as he took a deep breath. 'The British Government has apparently decreed that this proud nation, forged in adversity, is now surplus to requirements.'

A buzz of incomprehension rose from the crowd and on a balcony two dusty, camouflaged figures looked down at him; then Delgado sang.

'*Hey man, cut the shit and get to it.*'

Baxter held his hands up in surrender. 'I am, Delgado, I am. They want to evacuate the island. They want you to pack your possessions, leave your homes and move to another island. Apparently they have jobs for you there.

But you have to leave in three weeks.'

There was no reaction, just hundreds of blank stares. The Union Jacks still fluttered and Baxter began to get annoyed.

'Did you understand what I said? Don't you have any questions?'

Only one. From behind him. His wife.

'Sure. Why can't we leave tomorrow?'

For the first time in years Baxter felt wide awake and tense and he didn't like the feeling. He stood leaning against the reception room looking out into the night, while behind him Pepito and Eric shared the rum bottle and a joint. Next door Nado was still trying to clear up the debris caused by a large chunk of the cannon, which had smashed through the window and ploughed into the dining table, set for eight, and had brought down the ceiling fan. He was lucky. He had been counting the spoons when it happened and the rusty iron had missed him.

The two policemen were not so lucky. They were in bunks in the doctor's surgery where their condition was said to be comfortable.

Baxter still couldn't believe what had happened. Where was the Government's sense of responsibility? What had happened to the promise on the passport and the security of being British?

All the things he had been taught at school had been thrown out the window. He was one of the elite, to be sure, but with his privileges came responsibility. He had had that lesson drilled into him and it was the main reason he did not leave Dolores. No matter how grotesque she became, he would never ditch her. He had made his vows after all, just a few weeks after they had met when the sex had still been amazing. Dolores had been very, very rude in those days, unlike the Samanthas and Arabellas he had known.

He would not ditch her because he was responsible for

56

her, just as Whitehall was responsible for the people of Cascara. What they were doing simply wasn't fair.

He turned to the others and nodded. 'I'll fight this, Pepito. But will the people back me up?'

Pepito shrugged. 'I'm not sure, Governor. Going away will give them jobs. Staying won't.'

'But this is their home,' he yelled, surprising them and himself with his passion.

Pepito just kept shrugging, as if he had epilepsy. 'People have left more beautiful islands than this to live in the Bronx.'

'Aye,' said Eric. 'The grass is always greener.'

Baxter was confused. His world had been made more complicated and reactions were not what they should have been.

'They'll find it a lot more expensive,' he said weakly.

'I have no desire for pastures new,' said Eric. 'I've avoided the real world for many years and I'm totally unprepared to return to it.'

Now it was Baxter's turn to shrug his shoulders. He leant against the wall and took a hit from Pepito, trying to get his brain into gear, frustrated by the deviousness of his superiors and the apathy of his inferiors.

Then came the sound of happiness, Dolores waltzing into the room carrying a hatbox and a sheaf of dresses on hangers.

She danced up to Baxter and kissed him on the cheek.

'You know, *mi amor*, when we get to England maybe the Queen reward you. She make you Lord Thwaites.' Her eyes sparkled. 'Lord and Lady Thwaites of London.'

Then she turned and danced back the way she had come.

'Deescoss,' she shouted. 'Partees. Arrods, Vidal Sassoon.'

Baxter watched her sadly. 'Dolores is taking it awfully well,' he said.

Seven

The first boat to dock at Port Agnes after the departure of the man from Whitehall was a small fishing smack out of St Vincent. The five-hour voyage had exhausted the three fishermen, not so much by the work of sailing the boat as by the regular trips below to relieve themselves, for none of the three men had ever seen anything quite like their passenger.

Pamela Weintraub was thirty years old and five feet nine inches of radiant optimism. She oozed health and vitamins, hope and enthusiasm. To many men, captivated by her beauty, her outlook on life proved in the end to be too much. She was almost inhuman.

As the boat approached the pier, she was standing in the bows and the fishermen stared at her as if she were a goddess. She turned and smiled at them. The sunlight flashed on her perfect teeth. Her golden hair, backlit by the sun, looked like a commercial for herbal shampoo, uncorrupted by chemical additives. As one, the three men crossed themselves and silently asked forgiveness for their unclean thoughts.

The voyage had not affected her. No perspiration had stained the four hundred dollar safari suit from Saks. The salt spray hadn't dimmed the shine on the Gucci boots.

They docked early to a seemingly deserted port and Pamela was the first onto the jetty, skipping along like some kind of young deer, searching in vain for Customs and Immigration, then turning to offer words of encouragement to the fishermen as they unloaded her bags.

She stopped at a tiny wooden hut and listened for the sound of movement. Someone was inside, someone, she thought, who would be of assistance. She knocked. A few minutes later the door opened and the oldest face she had ever seen looked out, the hands fumbling with trouser buttons.

'Oh, excuse me, I'm sorry to disturb you,' she said. The voice was uptown Manhattan, East Side, around the Nineties. She introduced herself and held out her hand. The old man squinted at it, wiped his hand on his trousers and shook it as if it were china.

She beamed at him, then stepped back and turned a complete revolution on one heel, threw her arms wide and closed her eyes. The old man had once been to a cinema aboard a troop ship and had seen his only movie. It was 'The Sound Of Music'. Patiently he waited for her to launch into 'The hills are alive...'

Instead she sighed.

'After New York,' she said, 'this place is like a breath of fresh air. Already I feel at home. Do you know how exciting it is to find a place so timeless and so... so elemental?'

The old man blinked and looked along the jetty to the square where the first of the women and children were congregating and peering at the new arrival. It was still too early for the men. Most of them would be sobering up. Then a shadow fell, and he looked up to see Pamela bending over him and was conscious of a smell of peppermint.

'Can you direct me to the nearest Hertz or Avis?' she asked...

An hour later Pamela was crushed in the back of Cascara's only bus, an open-top wreck that twice weekly made a tour of the island, stopping off at the shanties. It was no busier than usual, just seemed so to the locals because of six pieces of luggage, chocolate brown with a red-green stripe around each.

A baby squawled in her ear and dribbled milk. She smiled at it and patted its head. An old woman sat wedged against her, a fat thigh sweating against her slacks, a piglet squirming on her fat lap.

Pamela turned to her and smiled again.

'I love your pig,' she said. 'Does he have a name?'

'Dinner,' said the woman and Pamela had to suppress a groan. That old joke. She didn't think it would have arrived in Cascara already. In normal circumstances she would have kicked off her speech about the obscenity of eating the flesh of animals, but the look on the old woman's face discouraged it. Maybe later, she thought. You have to tread carefully with ancient cultures. She knew that from experience.

The bus lurched round a corner and she glimpsed a sign on the road, saying 'Government House: Garage Sale', and an arrow. She got to her feet, avoiding the eyes of the piglet, because she did not want to see them in her nightmares.

The visit of the man from Whitehall had stirred Government House into something approaching bustle and Baxter was saddened by the activity. The lawn reminded him of garden fetes from his youth but without the gaiety. Trestle tables had been set up haphazardly and overflowed with clothes and shoes, toiletries and cosmetics, magazines (but no books, he noticed: Dolores had a short attention span), a record collection of sambas and rumbas and tangos, an exercise bicycle and an ancient movie camera.

A group of women scavenged among the treasure and several old men squatted on the grass, sucking at pipes. It was a silent ritual shattered only by the occasional Guatemalan curse as Dolores haggled over prices and the indignity of being offered a tennis ball for a Balenciaga.

As Baxter wandered across the lawn, he noticed an old man greedily reading the *Beverly Hills Diet*. Must be

60

working, Baxter thought, for he was so thin you could spit through him.

He reached the house, wandered into the reception room and gazed dejectedly at the scene. Packing cases and tea-chests covered most of the floor space. Racks of dresses partitioned the room. A goat and a couple of chickens wandered in and out of view.

Pepito and Lucille looked up at him and nodded, then resumed the work of packing. Baxter shook his head, conscious of a terrible sense of waste. All those memories being packed away, pointless years governing something that was about to be returned to the care of nature.

A surge of anger passed through him and he fought it. Why bother? The population did not care and so why should he? But he knew that he was not grieving for them. It was for himself. He sniffed then scolded himself. No point moping. Best to get on with it. Stiff upper lip and all that.

He picked up an inventory and began to check the contents.

'Confidential files and accounts,' he said, slapping the side of a crate, then moving to another. 'Office machinery.' Then he squinted at the biggest crate of all in the middle of the room, already nailed down.

'What's in this one?'

'Mrs Thwaites' shoes, Governor,' said Pepito.

Baxter snorted. 'I'm not taking those through Customs. Put them on the banana boat.' Maybe, he thought treacherously, they'll go rotten, like the bananas.

He reached forward, bent from the waist and separated a rack of dresses to let in some light, and stared breast-high at a vision.

Pamela smiled. 'Hi.' A little squeaky sound.

Baxter blinked. He had never seen anyone so clean. Automatically he made comparisons with his wife. Where Dolores' skin was olive, this creature's was golden; where Dolores' hair was dark and greasy, this was light and fair; where Dolores scowled, this one smiled; and the smell was

61

different. She was gesturing to the door saying she had come in the back way.

'My name's Pamela Weintraub,' she said. 'I'm looking for the Governor.'

Baxter nodded and behind the dresses made a shushing gesture to Pepito who had joined him.

'Listen,' she said, 'before I see him, how do I address this guy? I mean, is it Your Excellency, or just plain sir, or what? You know how tight-assed the British can be.'

'Oh, he's a pretty easy-going chap,' Baxter said. 'I've even seen him around the house without his sword on.'

He gazed at her cleavage comparing her to Dolores, the golden skin, a gentle swell of flesh, pert little... Pamela caught his glance and threw it back at him, smiling as if flattered. There was a pause, a moment of silent eye contact. A spell was being cast and Pepito broke it.

'Why do you wish to see the Governor, miss?'

'I'm an environmental activist,' she said, turning to him. 'As soon as I heard about the evacuation of the island, I flew straight down. You see, I want to give it back to the bat.'

The two men were entranced, listening to her with their heads cocked, like birds.

'I'm referring to the long-eared horseshoe bat,' she said. 'This island used to be its natural habitat. Now that Man is leaving, they may once more flourish.'

Quite a speech, Baxter thought, then a movement to his left distracted him. The goat was halfway through a Bill Gibb.

'Oh shit,' he said. 'He's eating one of my wife's dresses.' He yelled at it to get out but Pepito took charge, going for the goat saying: 'I'll take care of it, Governor.'

Pamela slapped a hand against her forehead. 'Governor? I thought you were the removal men.'

Baxter made a small bow, then reached for her hand. It was cool and slightly moist, and he stifled an urge to lick it.

'Baxter Thwaites,' he said. 'I *am* that tight ass.'

'Oh boy, Pamela,' she said. 'You did it again.'

'I did help rather. The truth is, the days of British rule are just about to expire, so we don't stand on ceremony here.'

She nodded, drew her hand away and stepped back. 'I can see you're very busy. Why don't I come back later?' She glanced out the back door at the dirt track leading to the dirt road. 'Uh, where does one stay in Cascara?'

'One doesn't usually.'

'It doesn't have to be too fancy,' she said. 'I mean, like a Holiday Inn or a Howard Johnsons...'

'The best we can offer is Aunt Matilda's Guest House and Domino Club.'

Pamela looked doubtful. 'Does it have air-conditioning?'

'I don't think it has water,' he said, the obvious solution coming immediately to mind. 'I think you'd better stay here, Pamela, as the last official guest of the British Government.'

She beamed at him. 'That would be a privilege, Governor.'

'Baxter.'

She nodded and Baxter left her to sort out her luggage, then turned to Pepito.

'Can you ask the girls to prepare the guest room. I've asked Miss Weintraub to stay the night.'

'Who can blame you, Governor?' Pepito said.

Eight

For Rob Waring, the unscheduled trip back to Houston
was a massive gamble. By cancelling the commercial, he
had put his career on the line. He was flying by the seat of
his pants. He had made a unilateral executive decision,
off his own bat, as it were, and he could only pray that it
was the right decision.

On the plus side, he recalled Franklin Spender's dictum
that what he wanted was executives with minds of their
own. Hell, the big man had said that was the goddamn
dictionary definition of the word. Ex-ec-u-tive. He did not
need yes-men. The trouble was, no one had ever tested the
theory. Everyone said yes to Franklin Spender. It was
automatic. All Rob could pray for was that the big man
would reciprocate and say yes to him.

The first leg of the trip to Miami wasn't so bad, but in
the Lear jet taking him to Houston, Rob began to sweat.
The farther he got from Cascara, the nearer he got to
Houston, the more he realised how momentous was his
decision. Maybe he should have capped the well, finished
the commercial and mentioned the friggin' Perrier when
he got back; but that wasn't the stuff of dynamism; that
was hedging bets, the action of a wimp. All sorts of things
could happen. People could get drunk and talk, and then
Gulf or Texaco might nip in and steal his thunder.

No, the decision was the right one. He had made his bed
and now he would lie on it, and he could only pray that it

wasn't his death bed, career-wise.

In the limo from the airport Rob closed his eyes and conjured up the expression on Ben's face when the survey had been made. Between one and two billion barrels a year, he had said, which was as big as the offshore field in the Baja.

'This is a seat on the Board,' Rob had replied in the initial glow of enthusiasm. 'This is stock options. This is profit sharing. This is barbecues at Spender's ranch on Sundays.'

But the Texan wasn't so sure. He knew only oil, after all. 'If the old man doesn't buy it,' he had said, 'he might just barbecue you.'

On the way up in the elevator towards the executive floor beneath the penthouse – the penthouse itself being what Spender called his pied-à-terre and no one from Spenco was invited – Rob thought of himself turning on a spit with Spender's boys spooning on the sauce and the old man himself slicing steaks from his rump. He whistled to himself, trying to think what he would do if he failed. There were always other jobs, like a gas station attendant, or bus-boy, or an elevator operator.

The elevator boy looked at him with some sympathy. He knew that whistling was a sign of tension.

'Don't worry, sir,' he said and Rob grinned mirthlessly at him. Rumour had it that the elevator boy was once a director of marketing at Exxon . . .

Ten minutes later, Rob entered the ante-room to the boardroom and smiled at Spender's executive secretary, a woman of fifty who had been with the boss since she was eighteen. Like the room, she was spartan. There was no concession to personal taste, no furnishings that weren't functional, just understated affluence; the walls were Norwegian pine, the floor wall-to-wall English parquet.

Waring clicked across it, took a deep breath and went through the double doors into the inner sanctum. The others were already there. Arlene from marketing, Dr Jewison, the senior chemist, and three others he did not know. He had briefed Arlene and the chemist by phone and he could see that they had done the preparation work. On the boardroom table stood bottles of Perrier, Evian, Vichy Poland and Highland Spring, and a tray of glasses.

He nodded to each of them and looked around. Again, there was nothing fancy. On the far wall, a painting – in oil – of a rig in the North Sea being buffeted by forty-foot waves, the rig's lights done in electric bulbs, winking on and off. On the wall behind Spender's chair a picture of the great man, thumbs in his belt, stetson at an angle. It had been painted twenty years earlier, before the jowls had set to make him look like a giant spaniel, before the eyes had become slits from glowering at people, before the belly had overhung the belt.

Nothing was said. Rumour had it that the room was bugged, and rumours at Spenco were believed – implicitly.

A hiss as the door in the far wall opened and Franklin Spender stood for a moment, framed like his picture, then he moved quickly to his seat, tilted back his stetson and nodded to Rob. At least he didn't put his spurs on the table. That was something.

Rob went into his presentation, fighting to sound convincing, striving for confidence. When he finished, there was a five second silence, then Spender leant forward and glared at him.

'We struck this stuff in the fifties,' he growled. 'That's why we pulled out of Cascara.'

Lesser men would have run away, but Rob had his answer.

'In the fifties, Mr Spender, we didn't realise its commercial potential.' The 'we' was deliberate. Rob was born in the fifties. What he was doing was actually criticising the younger Franklin Spender for lack of foresight. It was the bravest sentence he had ever uttered.

'In the fifties,' he continued, 'nobody drank designer water.'

Spender leant further forward and Rob clenched his

66

buttocks, forced himself not to look away, then the chemist was mercifully on his feet, reading from a report. Spender, however, did not shift his gaze.

'The water has one unique quality which separates it from other proprietary brands,' said the chemist. 'According to our lab report, it has an aperient element which makes it cathartic.'

'What is that in English, Waring?' Spender barked.

'It helps you shit like clockwork, sir.'

Spender leant back, eyes shaking his head. 'You're asking me to market a laxative?'

At the word 'market', Arlene got to her feet. 'This could be a sales plus, sir,' she said. 'A situation has evolved in the eighties where the combined effect of junk food and urban stress has clogged up the bowels of America.'

Spender got to his feet and stood by the window, looked out for a moment then turned and shook his head.

'I'm an oil man,' he said. 'Water is so . . .' he searched for the word, '. . . gutless. Spenco strides the world like a colossus with a barrel of crude under each arm, not like some limp-wristed faggot with a glass of mineral water and a twist.'

Rob had only two more cards to play and so he played it, aware that this was the moment of truth. He reached into his briefcase, pulled out a can of motor oil and placed it next to a bottle of mineral water.

'This is our top-selling motor oil, sir, retailing at one dollar and seven cents. This bottle of imported French mineral water has an average price of a dollar seventy-nine. We don't have to refine our water. All we have to do is stick it in a fancy bottle and put a pretty label on it.'

Spender sniffed, reached for the unlabelled bottle – the Cascaran water – poured himself a glass and tasted it. Rob waited. No reaction. Then: 'How do the numbers stack up, Waring?'

And here came the trump card. 'I estimate we can make a clear profit of, let's say . . . six to seven hundred per cent.'

Spender nodded, briefly closed his eyes, then opened

them and said the words that made Rob Waring the happiest man in Texas.

'Gentlemen. We're in the water business.'

Nine

The arrival of Pamela Weintraub had done a lot to raise Baxter's spirits. That morning, when he awoke, he drowsily thought of a proverb and couldn't quite get hold of it; something about ill winds blowing no good, or some such thing. Dolores snored beside him and Baxter hastily swung himself out of bed, trying not to think about Pamela in the close vicinity of his wife. Somehow it was a betrayal of his marriage vows.

As he showered and shaved, the proverb came back and he smiled into the mirror. If Cascara hadn't been raped by Whitehall, then she wouldn't have come and he wouldn't be taking her round the island before lunch. He took a deep breath and felt glad to be alive. Not almost, but really glad.

She was already up and waiting for him by the Land Rover, a camera and binoculars round her neck and a map in her hand, smiling hello at him.

He drove west as far as he could then they walked the rest of the way towards the cliffs. The higher they climbed, the stronger the wind blew, until they were forced to bend into it. At the clifftop Baxter stopped her with a hand on her arm and pointed out the geography.

'This is the Atlantic side of the island,' he said, shouting to make himself heard. 'Not the most hospitable of places.' He pointed north. 'That's Depression Bay and across there is Point Peril.'

'I love it,' she said, and Baxter wasn't surprised. Pamela, he guessed, was in love with the whole planet. She took a deep breath. 'The solitude reminds me of Nova Scotia.'

Why on earth, he wondered, would anyone go to Nova Scotia?

'I was defending baby seals.'

Of course, he thought, I should have known.

'I wasn't there too long,' she said. 'I'd only been protesting for two hours when they had to fly me to hospital in Halifax.'

'Frostbite?' Baxter wondered.

'No.' She shook her head, a mass of blonde hair, and Baxter wondered what it would look like on a pillow. 'What happened was ... a hunter clubbed me on the head and a mother seal bit my ass.'

Baxter grinned. 'It sounds as though neither side appreciated your intentions.'

'That's what Howard used to say. Howard Weintraub, my ex-husband.'

Baxter said 'aah', a riddle solved. He'd wondered how someone so hundred per cent WASP could have a name like Weintraub.

'He's another of my lost causes,' she continued. 'We met defending the rights of migrant grape pickers. Then his values changed and he went into cable television.'

'Howard's loss is the bats' gain, Pamela,' said Baxter but she wasn't listening. She was scanning the area with her binoculars and Baxter waited patiently for her to finish and start talking again, because he liked the sound of her voice and enjoyed her adolescent sense of wonder, but when she spoke there was a hardness of tone he hadn't heard before.

'You never told me Spenco was on the island.'

He noticed that her binoculars were aimed at the rig. 'Don't worry,' he said, 'they're not raping the environment.' He was pleased that such a modern phrase had sprung so easily to mind after all these years in the middle of nowhere. 'They've been using that old rig to shoot a commercial.'

She lowered the binoculars and handed them across. 'So why do they have a chainlink fence and guards with baseball bats?'

He took them and gazed through them. She was right. It was what she might have called a very heavy scene down there, some kind of armed camp.

'Now what are they up to?' he wondered aloud. He lowered the glasses and shrugged, his first reaction being: so what? It was no longer any of his business. Then he turned and saw Pamela looking at him and challenging him. She was right. He'd have to check it out. If not for Whitehall, if not for the Cascarans, for the fact that Pamela Weintraub was expecting it of him. Chest puffed, bristling with official outrage, he strode towards the fence.

Rob Waring was so pleased with himself that he celebrated with champagne on the flight south, then, on an impulse, decided to make the last stage of the journey by powerboat, to get some salt spray on his face and sea air in his lungs. During the trip he happily went over and over the memory of his success. When Spender had left, his back had been slapped and his hand shaken. The big man hadn't yet mentioned barbecues at his ranch but maybe Rob was being premature. Wait till the first sales reports came in; that would be the time.

Cascara, as it appeared on the horizon, seemed to him to be a dream island. Never mind the clouds and the black volcano. To Rob it was like Bali or Maui, or Praslin in the Seychelles. It was the Garden of goddamn Eden, that's what it was. He let out a whoop, startling the skipper, and danced a little jig, watching the island take shape, thinking of Ben, somehow needing the big Texan's handshake and his seal of approval.

This was what he was all about, getting a profit-making

concern under way, not acting as wet-nurse to some over-the-hill actor.

The little port and the jetty seemed like home to him as he shook hands with the skipper and stepped jauntily ashore, feeling like a sailor home from the sea, his briefcase in one hand, his overnight bag on his shoulder like a kit-bag. There was even a welcoming party – Pepito and the two policemen, still in their bandages.

He smiled at them but they did not smile back, and he was reminded of expressions he had seen at airports and docks the world over. No, he thought. Couldn't be. It must be his imagination. But it wasn't.

'Customs and Immigration, Mr Waring,' said Pepito sternly.

'Hey guys,' said Rob, smile still in place. 'You know my face. I really have to get to the site...'

'We insist,' said Pepito, interrupting him.

Rob shrugged as he was ushered towards the Customs shed. He hadn't really noticed it before, just thought it was some sort of old shack, but there was the Union Jack flying above it and the sign newly painted over the door.

'Give an Arab a stripe,' he muttered angrily at Pepito's back, unaware that the man was known for his keen sense of hearing.

In the next few minutes, his irritation turned to anger and then to humiliation. He seethed, sitting in his boxer shorts and singlet, his initials as red as his face, as Pepito and the policemen went through his bag and his briefcase. He clenched his fists and plotted revenge, thinking that only a matter of hours ago he had sold water to Franklin Spender and now, he was reduced to this...

A shadow fell across him and he looked up into the face of Baxter Thwaites.

'Governor,' he beamed, getting to his feet, 'am I glad to see you. Do you see what these goons are putting me through?'

Baxter turned and watched the proceedings, then

looked back at Rob. Like Pepito, he wasn't smiling. 'These goons, Mr Waring,' he said. 'represent Her Majesty's Customs and Immigration.'

Rob blinked and wondered what had got into the man. The psychology course at Spenco hadn't prepared him for the niceties of dealing with natives, or the governors of natives. As far as Houston was concerned, American Express always did the trick, or in the case of the more primitive types, the good old greenback. Maybe he should have tipped the Governor last time out; but, even as he was considering the possibility, he saw one of the goons tipping out the contents of his toilet bag, and his sense of outrage returned.

This was too much. This was private. He pointed at the man, his arm trembling with rage.

'Those are my vitamins,' he squealed. 'B stress, Niacin and Ginseng. And I have a prescription for those tranquillisers.'

But no one took any notice. It was as if he did not exist, and now Pepito was opening a memo from his briefcase and saying to Baxter that it was interesting.

'Hey,' Rob yelled again. 'Those are highly confidential documents.'

Now they had really gone over the top. This would mean an official complaint. He would get onto the State Department about this. He would get onto the fuckin' Marines, was what he would do.

Baxter sniffed. 'What's the bottom line, as our American cousins would say?'

Pepito was still reading. 'I haven't perused the small print,' he said, 'but it would appear that Spenco is trying to screw the British Government.'

Rob froze in his underpants as four pairs of eyes gazed at him in accusation. He thought he had gone through the gamut of emotions, but there was one remaining. He panicked.

An hour later, dressed once more and sitting with a glass of rum outside the Marimba Bar, the panic had

eased and had been replaced by dejection, as he wondered
how long it would take him to master the elevator job. He
never had been any good with machines.

All around him were signs of the evacuation. A store
keeper was loading a cart. Another was nailing planks of
wood across a window. Rob barely noticed. Everything
seemed to be happening in slow motion; even Baxter
sounded far off as he spoke to him. The Governor was
friendly now that Rob had been stripped of his arrogance.
He was no longer a threat and Baxter felt sorry for him.
He was like a defeated dog who offers his throat to the
winner, and so Baxter was gentle with him.

'What you overlooked,' he said as he poured a slug of
rum into the American's glass, 'before you scurried off to
Texas, was that Spenco's drilling rights expired in...
when was it?'

Pepito, at his side, supplied the date from his clipboard:
October 17, 1976.

'And until you've negotiated an extension,' Baxter
continued, 'your case isn't really watertight.' He smiled at
his little joke. 'So I think you'll agree, old sport, we have
you over a barrel.'

'Apparently two million barrels,' said Pepito.

'Cheers,' said Baxter and raised his glass.

'Cheers,' repeated Rob glumly. 'My career's down the
toilet.'

Baxter let him suffer for a few seconds before saying:
'Not necessarily.'

Rob looked up, and Baxter continued:

'Maybe we can make a deal.'

The word zipped into the most active part of Rob's
brain.

'Deal? Yeah, we can make a deal.'

Deals were what Rob was all about.

'You want to keep your job,' said Baxter. 'I want jobs for
these people. Then they won't have to leave the island.'

The fog of dejection lifted to be replaced by enthusiasm.

'I can use them,' he said happily. 'Cheap labour, right

here on the spot. No unions. Boy, can we deal!'

Baxter bent and glared at him. 'You are not going to *use* them, Mister Waring. They're not going to stick labels on bottles for three dollars a month. They'll have realistic wages, and social and medical benefits.'

Details, thought Rob, and agreed readily. Anything to keep the deal open. 'Only fair, Governor,' he said. 'We're talking about human beings here.'

'And some of the profits will be ploughed back into things this island needs.'

'Like a school,' said Pepito. 'And a hospital.'

Rob felt like the Dutch guy who bought Manhattan off the Indians. 'You got it,' he said, his training standing him in good stead now. What was needed was a show of good faith for these schmucks. A bonus to keep them happy. 'And we'll throw in a video arcade,' he said, looking into Baxter's face, seeing nothing. 'Now, how do we fix these drilling rights?'

'Hopefully with one phone call,' said Baxter.

Sir Malcolm had deliberately steered clear of the luxurious La Toc Hotel in the bay south of Castries. Instead he had rented two apartments on the Morne, high above the port. You couldn't be too careful these days. The atmosphere had changed radically since old Cecil had found himself in the khazi and, of course, the PM was not known for being, shall we say, the most liberal of leaders.

It was just elementary diplomacy to keep a low profile, and besides, he had a brass bedstead, solid and dependable, which he could clutch with both hands, just like the one he had as a boy when his nanny would ...

His reverie was interrupted by Sarah's anxious voice.

'Um, I don't wish to be impertinent, Sir Mal, but aren't we rather over-extending our trip? Not that I'm not having a super time.'

He sighed. Half-asleep on the lilo by the pool, with Sarah massaging the Ambre Solaire into his back, he had quite forgotten how incredibly thick she was.

75

'Sarah, my dear,' he said, vaguely aware that he was using the same patronising tone he had perfected for Marjory. 'They don't expect us back until the evacuation of Cascara is complete. You typed the memo, remember?'

'Oh, gosh. So I did. Yah.'

He sighed and closed his eyes then twitched as the phone rang by his head. He grabbed the receiver and smacked it against his ear, wondering if it was trouble. Only the office, Marjory and Cascara had the number. When he heard the name Thwaites, he grunted with relief.

'What is it?' he snapped. 'I'm under savage pressure here.'

He placed his hand over the mouthpiece and turned. 'A little lower, Sarah,' he whispered, and she obliged. Sarah's dumbness had its compensations. She was totally obedient.

He turned back to the phone and screwed up his face, the better to comprehend what the silly man was saying. It all sounded incredibly trivial.

'The Yanks have found what? ... Water?' God, he thought, what next? Couldn't Thwaites do his job without jumping on the phone every five minutes? 'Yes of course you have my authority to extend their mining rights. London takes the view that everything on that island is for sale or lease. Why don't you see if you can get a good price for the volcano while you're at it?' And he slammed the phone down, chuckling at his joke.

Water indeed!

'Is there a hiccup?' Sarah asked.

'Nothing for you to worry your little head about,' he said. 'Why don't you make us both one of those drinks with an umbrella in it?' Her hands pressed into his spine and gave him an idea. 'And then perhaps you could slip into that costume.'

Obedient as always, she got to her feet. 'The nurse or the naughty schoolgirl?' she asked.

Briefly he felt a tremor of disappointment. Why was it always he who had to make the decisions?

76

'I think the latter,' he said, turning to watch her walk up the stairs towards her room. She had beautiful legs.

'And Sarah,' he said. 'Don't forget the knee socks.'

She turned and pouted at him, already motivating herself into her role.

Ten

For once there was a legitimate reason to get the champagne out. Baxter stood in the middle of the reception room and ceremoniously popped the cork, a tiny echo of the gusher that had come to the aid of the island. He filled the glasses of Rob and Pepito, then leant forward, rested the contract against the figurehead and signed it, vaguely conscious of a sigh of delight from the American. That done, he handed it over and offered the pen, over his forearm as if it were a sword. Rob signed. Then it was Pepito's turn. He could hardly contain his excitement. This was what he had learned the Queen's English for, to be permitted to witness history, officially. It was just a pity that the Governor hadn't asked him to make a speech.

It was done. The three men raised their glasses and chorused a toast: 'To Cascara'.

At that, the door opened and Pamela exploded into the room like a warm breeze, her cheeks flushed with excitement. It made Baxter feel healthy, just looking at her.

'Baxter,' she said, 'I was walking near Cape Despair when I saw my first bat.'

He was about to congratulate her when Rob butted in with a: 'Hi, Pamela'.

She turned and stared at him, her excitement evaporating as if she had just fallen into a snowdrift.

'Waring, what are you doing here?' she asked aggressively, as if he had no right to be breathing the same air, and all Baxter could say rather feebly was, 'Have you two met?'

'We've crossed swords, yes,' said Pamela.

'Wasn't that the time when you were picketing our toxic waste dumps in West Virginia?' Rob asked.

Pamela nodded, straightening her shoulders and pushing out her chest. 'Thanks to me, fish can once more swim in the Ohio River.'

'Thanks to Spenco,' said Baxter, 'the island is saved. They're going to give us an industry.'

Pamela glared at him and he backed off a step. He had only ever been the recipient of her smile and he didn't like the transformation.

'Then I have no choice,' she said. 'I shall fight you. Just give me a moment to pack my things.'

She turned and made for the door but Baxter was too fast, running round and confronting her, telling her he did not understand.

'You're in league with the devil, Baxter,' she said. 'I have been fighting Franklin Spender since I was three.'

And Baxter giggled at the absurdity of the idea. 'How on earth did he upset you at that age?' he asked. 'Was he manufacturing defective teddy bears?'

'Franlin Spender manufactured defective families,' she said, glaring at him. 'Franklin Spender is my father.'

And for once in his life Baxter Thwaites was speechless.

Ten minutes later Baxter pulled up at the foot of the hill leading to Radio Cascara and ran up. He was panting slightly and, for the hundredth time, made a vow to get rid of his paunch. The only problem was how. The sea was a living minefield. There were no tennis courts or swimming pools and he was no jogger. They would have thought him mad and any authority he might have had would vanish.

Maybe he could get Spenco to build a pool. It was an idea. He made a mental note to mention it to Waring.

Jay Jay greeted him warmly. The Dee Jay was not a

man to bear grudges. Maybe he might if he could remember the grudge for any length of time, but the ganja had played havoc with his memory. He was so honoured by the visit that he did something unique. He interrupted Bob Marley.

'Attention all Cascarans,' he said. 'Governor Thwaites has an important announcement to make.'

He cued him in and sat back as Baxter leant towards the mike.

'Friends,' he said, 'I have great news...'

Throughout the port, heads were cocked towards their radios and, in the Marimba Bar, Eric McNab's hand fluttered over the draught he was about to play. He was going to beat Miguel for once, but the voice of the Governor signalled an adjournment.

'Fortune has smiled upon us,' Baxter continued. 'Spenco, an equal opportunity employer, has jobs for all able-bodied men and women right here on the island.'

Jay Jay, scanning the town, saw no sign of movement, which was a good sign. It meant that the people were paying attention.

'Top wages in US dollars,' said Baxter. 'Bonus incentives, medicare and pension plans. Sign up tomorrow at Vasco da Gama Recreation Centre. Recruitment begins at nine a.m.'

A murmur of approval rippled through the port, punctuated by only one voice of dissent, a blonde head, poking out from the top floor window of Aunt Matilda's Guest House and Domino Club, shouting:

'Don't sell out. This is Coca-colonialism.'

Pamela shook her head and her hair swung in a perfect arc, attracting the attention of a group of men outside the bar. They nudged one another and made rude signs with palms and forearms, but only to themselves, and not in view of the lady.

The only other object of dissent was waddling up the hill towards the radio station as fast as her three-inch stilettos would permit.

Inside, Jay Jay was slapping palms with Baxter and telling him that he was the boss-govnah-boss-man, but the smile froze on his face as the door was kicked open. Dolores did not wait for an invitation. She was jittery with hysteria, a hundred and forty pounds of female time bomb on a short fuse. The wrong answer from her husband would light it.

'Baxter,' she said softly. 'Tell me you keed me. Tell me you mehk yoke. You say we no leave, ha ha, very funny. April Fool.'

Baxter lit the fuse. 'The situation has changed, Dolores. We have to stay.'

'Aieeee,' she said, rushing at him, knocking records to the floor. Baxter staggered back against the console, stumbled and reached out blindly, hitting the microphone key so that his wife's scream of outrage was transmitted across the island.

'So, Baxter, once more you lie to me.'

In the Marimba Bar, the draughts game was adjourned for a second time.

'What do you mean, once more?'

'You lie to me when I was a girl in Guatemala.'

She lunged for him and Baxter ducked away, pushing Jay Jay aside, unaware of his whisper that the mike was on.

'You weren't a girl,' he said, instinctively working on the strategy of attack being the best form of defence. 'You were *never* a girl.'

'I was eennocent,' she squealed. 'You beguiled me. You say I be wife of deeplomat. You say I geeve cocktail parties and launch sheeps.'

In Government House, Nado, Pepito and Lucille formed a small scrum around the radio set, Pepito and Lucille looking shocked, Nado smiling.

'Let's face it, Dolores,' Baxter said. 'You never fitted into diplomatic life.'

'Oh, so you say I embarrass you. You are ashamed by me.'

Again Jay Jay made a grab for the key but Dolores pushed him away into a stack of records.

'I'm just saying,' Baxter answered, striving to remain calm, 'that things might have turned out differently if you hadn't danced the Cucaracha topless at that Embassy reception for the Duke of Edinburgh.'

'He loved it.'

'So much so, we were sent to Cascara.'

For a moment Jay Jay thought that Missus Governor was about to smash the place up, including Mistah Governor and his good self. She was teetering on the brink. Destruction or self-destruction. The balance shifted from one to another in her mind, while the two men waited helplessly for the outcome.

Then: '*Adios*, Baxter,' she said quietly. '*Adios* forever. I go now. I keel myself.'

She turned and marched out, brushing away a tear, leaving Jay Jay blinking in relief, while a mile away a cheer echoed round Government House and Nado ran to the kitchen to sharpen a machete.

Only two men on the island were unaware of the news, Delgado's radio being permanently tuned to Radio Havana. They sat outside their hut, feeding off one another's despair. Garfield was cooking stew in a black pot and Delgado was sitting cross-legged, gazing blankly at the horizon, thinking of the eviction of his people. He could not even console himself with the fact of being right. There was no point in saying: 'I told you so', to people who did not care. They were sheep, dumbly prepared to be herded off to some capitalist playground to act as flunkeys in monkey suits.

Sheep, monkeys; not worth fighting for. Fidel was right. They were too downtrodden even for him. It was sad, and the saddest thing of all to Delgado was that now, at the age of whatever-he-was, he knew he would never see Moscow.

There was a crackling in the bushes and he looked up,

into the eyes of the most beautiful woman he had ever seen, but he felt nothing. Delgado had taken a vow of celibacy with his vow of silence, and he was well-known for being strict with his vows. Garfield, on the other hand, stopped stirring his stew and began to dribble at the mouth.

The vision introduced herself and they waited for her to continue. She smiled at one, then the other.

'You must be the one they call the Singing Rebel, and you're Garfield, his lieutenant and bongo player.'

She offered her hand to Delgado and he reached for it without getting up. It was an odd sort of handshake and he nearly broke his thumb trying to disentangle himself. A flash of memory surfaced, of his father telling about the Freemasons, but they were all men, he remembered; unless things had changed.

Then she stood back and gazed over their shoulders at the shack.

'I love your home,' she said and sighed. They turned and looked at it, trying to see it through her eyes. 'It's a statement,' she added. Then: 'Tell me, do you rent or buy?'

They turned and blinked at her. She waited for them to speak, then slapped her palm against her forehead.

'Of course. I've heard. You won't speak until your people are free.' She shook her head, the smile widening until Delgado wondered how she could possibly speak through it. 'That's beautiful! I hear what you're saying. I mean, I hear what you're not saying. Your silence is eloquent.'

Delgado indicated an old chair and she perched on it. He was thinking that maybe she had been sent to hunt for them and that perhaps she was some kind of infiltrator; not that it mattered. There was nothing to infiltrate.

'You heard the news about Spenco?' she asked. No response. 'It's the perfect scenario. Now you have a focus. A target. Freedom fighters taking on the might of American Big Busines. I want you to know that I'm with you.'

To Delgado, this sounded interesting. If he could have

spoken, he would have asked her to explain. Instead he snapped his finger at Garfield and nodded at the pot. Garfield took the hint and spooned some stew onto a cracked plate and handed it to her.

'I'm with you all the way,' she repeated into Delgado's face, taking the plate without thinking, concentrating hard on his reaction; then the smell hit her nostrils and she looked down at the stew and frowned.

'Is this salted? Because I'm on a sodium-free diet.'

Jesus Christ, said Delgado, but only to himself.

The Reverend McNab stood in the square watching the Cascarans file past the Spenco recruitment table, signing their names on the payroll, and he was reminded of a story he had read about the war, when a group of men from the Seychelles were conscripted to fight in the North American desert. The survivors learned two things: how to wear boots and the existence of homosexuality.

Eric grinned to himself; that was war and this was peace. If these innocents were to be corrupted, it would only be by a wage packet, and only a romantic dreamer could think that that was a bad thing.

He wandered across to talk to Rob Waring who was shouting through a bullhorn, encouraging the onlookers to join the line.

'Congratulations, Mister Waring,' he said. 'This will be the salvation of our island.'

Rob put down the bullhorn and smiled at him. 'Spenco has a heart, Rev.' Then he winced as the air was rent with the howl of amplified feedback, a painful, discordant cacophony coming at them from all angles.

Eric slapped his hands over his ears and groaned, recognising the all too familiar sound of a guitar being tuned up. He spun on one heel, searching for the source, and saw an amplifier in a tree, another on a roof and a third in a dustcart. Then someone was shouting and pointing. He looked up and groaned again, seeing his son on the balcony of Aunt Matilda's with a microphone set up in front of him and Garfield by his side with his keyboard.

'Oh God,' he said with feeling as Delgado hit a chord, yelled: 'CASCARA' and began to sing.

'I feel shame
I feel sad
I see my people
Act so bad,
Hear me scream
Hear me holler
You sell your soul
For a yankee dollar...'

Beneath him a door opened and Pamela rushed out, yelled encouragement at him, then turned to address the crowd, arms raised, breasts heaving.

'Listen to him. He's a home boy. He's a brother. He's your main man.'

Delgado took his cue and went into the chorus, a litany of protest:

'No no never no more
Never no more no never...'

As the crowd began to sway to the rhythm, Rob turned to Eric.

'Who the hell is that?' he asked.

'Huh?' Eric took his hands from his ears and Rob repeated the question.

'That's my son, my son,' he said sadly.

'You're his father, father?'

Eric nodded. 'A moment of weakness, many years ago. I was driven to sin by the solitude and the wind.'

Delgado's song brought Miguel and his men running into the square.

'No no never no more...'

'Can't you shut that bastard up?' Rob demanded of the Chief of Police, the word 'bastard' showering him with spittle. Miguel blinked and shook his head.

'Under British law,' he said officiously, 'singing badly is not a crime.'

Rob cursed, then once again illustrated why he had risen so quickly through the ranks of Spenco. He raised the bullhorn and turned to the crowd.

'A hundred dollars to the man who nails him.'

There was a moment's hesitation while they translated the word 'nail', then they rushed forward as one, surging towards Aunt Matilda's, while Manuel was struggling with his holster, trying to drag out his gun. British justice was British justice, he was thinking, and a hundred dollars was a hundred dollars.

On the balcony Delgado beamed.

'See my people
Come to me
All they want
Is lib-er-teee!'

But Garfield, as ever the practical one, knew better.

'All they want is our backside, man,' he said as Manuel's first bullet tore through the roof showering them with splinters.

It was another moment of humiliation for Delgado but he wasn't about to wallow in it. Unplugging his guitar, abandoning the amplifier for the moment, he scurried after Garfield, along the balcony and over the roof, boots clattering on corrugated tin, slithering onto the balcony at the back. They looked down and saw two bicycles parked side by side.

Delgado had once seen a Western on a troopship and he knew what to do. He nudged Garfield and they leapt together for freedom, but the saddles were harder than those on a horse and, as they landed, they knew from experience that the pain of impact, like the stubbing of a toe, is nothing compared to the agony afterwards, and when the crowd found them they were slumped, wheezing, heads on the handlebars and in no condition to resist arrest...

The jailhouse consisted of one small room partitioned by bars. By the time Baxter arrived, the two revolutionaries had recovered enough to stand, gripping the bars, and staring defiantly out at their jailer.

'Don't make me do this,' Baxter pleaded. 'Give me your word that you won't create a public nuisance and you're free.'

Garfield shook his head. 'The Rebel says we would rather stay here forever.' The tone of his voice made Baxter think that the little man was the weak link but at the moment he was reluctantly following his leader. Delgado, by contrast, was firm. There was nothing more unshakeable than martyrdom. Baxter sighed.

'Very well, have it your way. If you're going to stay here forever, you can finish the painting.'

The door opened and Pamela strode in. Anger, Baxter thought, made her look gorgeous. She ignored him and flattened herself against the bars, hands on hips.

'If those men are being locked up,' she declared, 'so should I be.'

'We don't have women's facilities,' he said.

'That's typically sexist.'

Baxter sighed again and tried a threat. 'I could deport you as an undesirable alien.'

The threat failed. She ignored it and turned to Delgado. 'I'm informing Amnesty International, and the media. Soon everyone will know your name. And the world will sing your music.'

'His lyrics don't rhyme,' warned Baxter.

She looked over her shoulder at him in contempt.

'The truth rarely does,' she said.

There was no answer to that and Baxter left, feeling defeated.

In Houston the campaign was in full swing. Franklin Spender strode around his office, a phone at his jaw, selecting advertising material from a range presented to him by a group of nervous ad-men. He liked the idyllic poster, the volcano set in a sparkling sea, spouting mineral water, with the legend: 'CASCARA – A SPA IS BORN'.

And he liked the small bottle, with a kind of oval feel to

it; like an Oilers football, it fitted nicely into his palm.

'Rob,' he roared into the phone. 'Research shows that this could be bigger than frozen yoghurt. So I want that bottling plant operational as soon as possible.'

In his ear, Rob Waring squeaked encouragement, only to be silenced by another roar of exhortation.

'Don't take that *mañana* crap. Do what we did in Aruba. Spike their coffee with amphetamine.'

He slammed down the phone leaving Rob Waring, two and half thousand miles to the south-east, perspiring with admiration and gazing at the receiver, thinking that it was just such attention to detail that made Spenco great.

Eleven

The idyll was over, lost in time and space, and within the
hour Sir Malcolm knew that he was to be called to
account. All that remained of the trip as evidence were
Sarah's scratches on his back which would have been
hard to explain to Marjory, but mercifully she had long
ago lost interest in removing his pyjama top.

If it were only that, he mused, as the car took him
through the drizzle towards the House. The radio was
blaring, great bellowings and guffaws punctuated by the
cries of the Speaker, demanding Order, Order, and not
getting it. Then there was a hush. This would be the PM
getting to her feet. Sir Malcolm closed his eyes and
shivered. She was always at her best when she was in
trouble, a born street-fighter when up against adversity,
so much so that some thought she welcomed it. But Sir
Malcom knew better, and what was horrible to con-
template was the fact that he had conjured up this
particular moment of adversity. It was all his damned
fault.

'I can assure the House,' she was saying, 'that the terms
due to our government in exchange for Cascaran mining
rights are both realistic and generous.'

The howls of derision from the Opposition benches
made Sir Malcolm cringe, and as the car swept through
the gates of Parliament, he felt as though he were sitting
in a tumbril.

An hour later he was ushered into the inner sanctum.

Whether she had kept him waiting by accident or design he could not know, but the result was that it was a trembling, stuttering wretch that faced her, the more wretched because he knew that she despised weakness. She liked strength, so long as it was not strong enough to disagree. It was a well-known maxim. So long as one did one's job to the best of one's abilities, then one was okay. The problem was that, on this occasion, one had cocked it up.

She was seated straight-backed behind her desk, slitting the throats of envelopes with a paperknife. She was in blue again, the pearls a dull U-shape across her bosom and she had not bothered with the niceties, like asking how he was or saying good afternoon, or offering him a chair, and so he stood, back against the wall by the door, as if ready to bolt for safety, as if there could be any safety in running away from the Prime Minister. He was aware also that he was twisting the Cascara file into a sort of aeroplane shape and he wished he could stop; but he couldn't.

She had simply asked him to explain himself and he tried.

'You will recall, Prime Minister, that due to the underhand methods of the Americans, we were at the time unware of their discovery.'

'Quite,' she said.

Not good, thought Sir Malcolm. He didn't like the tone, but he had no choice but to continue.

'And this is perhaps reflected in the somewhat...' he searched for the word. There wasn't a right one. None would do because she knew. He settled for 'disappointing'.... 'the somewhat disappointing revenue which we can anticipate.'

'How much?'

It wouldn't come out. He couldn't even stammer. He shivered, took a deep breath and launched the figure at her. 'One cent for every hundred barrels.'

Zip. The paperknife was past his ear and twanging in

the door before he could blink. He hadn't even seen her draw back her arm.

'I take it,' he quivered, 'you're asking for my resignation, Prime Minister?'

'It's too late for that,' she said, confusing him. 'I have been informed, though not by you, that there is a subversive element on Cascara. A Delgado Fitzhugh.'

'Just one person,' Sir Malcolm said.

'There was only one Gandhi once,' she said scornfully. 'One anorexic little loony in a loincloth and we lost a whole sub-continent.'

She got up and walked round the desk and he had to fight to stop himself whimpering. 'What Cascara needs,' she said, 'is a revolution. And the first act of the new Republic will be to nationalise all local industries. That is; Yankee go home.'

Sir Malcolm didn't understand and said so. 'I don't see,' he stammered, 'how that helps us.'

'Of course you don't,' she snapped. 'So let me make this absolutely clear. You will return to Cascara and secretly finance their revolution in exchange for a promissory contract guaranteeing us the bloody bottling rights.'

And he was dismissed; without pride, without the power of speech, but at least with his job. All that had to be done now was to get to Cascara soonest, which meant no hanging around waiting for scheduled flights. This was an RAF-RN job. Sarah pouted when she learnt she couldn't come and looked mutinous, and just for a moment Sir Malcolm had the waking nightmare that she was going to do to him what old Cecil's bird had done to Cecil. He trembled at the thought, as he said there-there and fondled her, thinking that if she were to turn nasty, it would be a John Stonehouse job; off with the three-piece suit and a swim to Australia.

But she was pacified with the promise of a weekend in the country soon. Within ten minutes the arrangements were made, the telegram to the Governor dictated, and he was off.

Baxter Thwaites was a happy man as he surveyed the interior of Government House. It was back to normal once more, everything unpacked and restored to its former place. He felt at home, and what was more, he felt fulfilled. He had done something useful. Not that anyone would thank him, but maybe one day they would realise, and he wondered where they would put the statue...

Sir Malcolm's message lay crumpled where he had dropped it. There would be no ceremonial uniform this time, no attempt at a welcome. Baxter was back in his shorts and quite looking forward to lording it over the little pipsqueak.

The drone of an engine made him look out. It was a Royal Navy helicopter coming in low over the scrub. For a moment it hovered over the lawn, the blades stiffening the Union Jack and battering the shutters against the wall. Then slowly it descended and Sir Malcolm stepped out, clutching a briefcase and a small overnight suitcase.

Baxter sauntered to the doorway and met Pepito, leant against the frame and watched Sir Malcolm march towards them. He had made no concession to the heat, wearing the same three-piece worsted pin-stripe, wax collar and school tie. All that's missing, thought Baxter, is the brolly, then he stumbled sideways as Dolores pushed past him and wobbled down the steps. She had dressed for the occasion in her best suit and stilettos, her cleavage smeared with baby oil, a pill-box hat pinned to her hair. She carried a suitcase and hat-box and shouted 'Wait for me' at the helicopter.

Brushing past Sir Malcolm, ignoring him as if he were invisible, she tottered towards the helicopter, then squealed in horror as it began to rise.

'Oh no,' she yelled, dropped her case and ran, arms wide in supplication, but the pilot had his orders and they did not include a passenger. It rose twenty feet and banked east as Dolores sank to her knees, arms raised as if in prayer, her screams slicing through the drone of the engine.

'Tekk me weeth you. Pliss. Oh, *Madre de Dios . . .*'

Then a terrible, pitiable sob as she realised she had lost and she beat her fists against her bosom, smearing her jacket in oil.

Sir Malcolm's nose wrinkled in disgust and he stepped back as far as he could from a scene of such gruesome emotion.

'Who on earth is that hysterical woman?' he said to no one in particular.

'My wife, Sir Malcolm,' said Baxter. 'She's a little overwrought. I think it's the strain of recent events.'

Sir Malcolm shuddered. 'For Gods sake have a word with her. That sort of thing doesn't do in front of the natives.' And he marched off into the house followed by Baxter and the glare of Pepito . . .

It was dark by the time Sir Malcolm had freshened up and they were into their second sundowner when he asked where Delgado was, the question taking Baxter by surprise; then, when he was told, Sir Malcolm produced the second surprise by asking to see him.

Ours not to reason why, Baxter thought as they drove to the jail. No doubt the man would explain when he was ready, or maybe not; after all, he had not even had the good grace to apologise for Whitehall's change of mind.

He led his guest up the steps to the jailhouse and stopped in the doorway, shaking his head at the sight that confronted them.

The cell door was open and Delgado and Garfield were sitting with Miguel on the wrong side of the bars, round a packing case that held the debris of their supper. The three men were playing cards, drinking rum and puffing on cigars, the smell of Havanas curdling with the stench of emulsion. A paint pot and two brushes stood by the cell door and three of the bars glistened green.

Miguel, seeing them, clumsily got to his feet, but Sir

Malcolm pushed his way into the room, patted his shoulder and told him not to get up.

Baxter felt the need to assert his authority in the face of such laxity.

'Miguel, why aren't these men under lock and key? They could walk straight out of here.'

'It's recreation hour, boss.'

Sir Malcolm nodded. 'Quite right too. Can't cage men up like animals.'

Baxter looked at him in surprise. The man was an enigma and untrustworthy at that, which was a dangerous combination. He watched, baffled, as Sir Malcolm patted Garfield's shoulder.

'How are they treating you, Delgado?' he asked. 'Got everything you need? Toothpaste? Tobacco?' He spotted a paint brush, grinned and picked it up. 'I see we're teaching you a trade. All part of the rehabilitation programme? Eh?'

Baxter interrupted with a diplomatic cough and made the introductions.

'Ah,' said Sir Malcolm, transferring his grin. Delgado glared at him, arms folded protectively high across his chest.

'How's the food then?' Sir Malcolm asked. No response. A moment of embarrassed silence. Sir Malcolm filled it by reaching across and lifting a spoonful. 'Looks jolly nourishing to me. What's it made from?'

'Betelwok, sir,' said Baxter. 'It's a local crop. From which the people make soup. Or rope. Depending on their needs at the time.'

'Good God.' He lowered it into the bowl as Miguel tried to press him, offering soup or rum, or whatever.

'Thank you, no,' said Sir Malcolm. 'What I really want is a word with these gentlemen alone.' He switched his attention to Baxter. 'Would you and the constable make yourself scarce for a moment?'

Curiouser and curiouser, thought Baxter as he took Miguel's arm and led him out. The Chief of Police went under protest and Baxter grinned at Sir Malcolm. He surely was making himself a bundle of enemies on the island, but it was par for the course. Hadn't the English been doing just that for centuries?

Baxter guided Miguel to a tree and together they leant against it, sharing a joint, the ganja easing the anger out of Miguel. There was no need to talk. Baxter meditated, quietly listening to the cicadas, enjoying the tranquillity. It was the best part of the evening, the hour before the mosquitoes woke up and got to work on them.

Peace and quiet. Baxter closed his eyes, took a long slow hit from the joint, then jumped, startled, at the *chung* of guitar strings from the jailhouse. The chord of G7, he reckoned, then a terrible roar from Delgado.

I can't believe
I'm sittin' in the jailhouse,
I can't believe
My ears is hearin'
What you say.

Then a strangled grunt and silence once more. Baxter and Miguel looked at one another and shrugged. Curiouser and curiouser.

Inside, Sir Malcolm had grabbed the neck of the guitar, cutting off Delgado's rhythm.

'For God's sake, man,' he whispered. 'There's no need to broadcast this all over the island. This is a highly secretive discussion, not *The Pirates of Penzance*.'

He dropped his hand as Delgado nodded.

'Let me spell it out for you,' he continued. 'In return for independence, all we ask is a fifty-fifty interest in the water. And you'll be President or Generalissimo, witch-doctor, whatever. You name the costumes, we'll provide the hats.'

Garfield tapped his arm and pointed to himself. 'Vice-President?' he asked.

'Absolutely, old chap,' said Sir Malcolm, beaming, realising he had found the weak link. 'And the next time there's a Royal Christening, you can pop over on a state visit. Front pew in the Abbey and tickets for Wimbledon.'

Garfield beamed but Delgado was still scowling.
Defiantly he battered out another chord and Sir Malcolm
twitched.

'You offer me fifty-fifty
You expect me to say yes
I'm a man of integritee
Sixty-forty!
No less!'

Sir Malcolm grabbed his strumming hand and shook
it.

'Done,' he said.

Baxter was finding it hard to believe what he was being
told. It was Machiavellian. It was Nixon and Kissinger at
their most devious. It was perfidious bloody Albion.

They were standing in the reception room, Sir Malcolm
chuckling to himself, shoulders twitching as he poured a
brandy. For once Baxter wasn't thirsty. The news made
him sick.

'Are you saying that this deal has the sanction of Her
Majesty's Government?' he asked incredulously.

'Perfectly orthodox ploy,' said Sir Malcolm. 'Bowing to
public opinion, we shall be forced to release the Rebel from
jail. Then he'll take to the hills with some bazookas and a
two-way radio, and we can start propagating the legend.
T-shirts, posters, that kind of thing.'

'This is beneath contempt,' said Baxter. 'You're
deciding a nation's fate without any regard for its
heritage or culture.'

Sir Malcolm sneered into his brandy glass. 'You call
rope soup a culture?'

And then he was asking where his room was. Curtly
Baxter gave him directions and walked out. He had
decided to take a drive round the island. He had a
hysterical wife and a devious little pipsqueak under his
roof and he wanted out. There was a smell about the place
as if something nasty had crawled in.

He slammed the door behind him, looked up at the volcano and cursed long and loud, words he thought he had long forgotten.

Twelve

Sir Malcolm couldn't sleep. It was too damned hot and the problem nagged at him. He told himself to think positively. He had found the Rebel and the deal had been struck, so the PM would be pleased. The trouble was that it was her idea and so she expected it to work. He would get no credit for it. He was on a hiding to nothing. He sighed. Maybe if she hadn't got such a large majority. Maybe if the Opposition weren't so damned inept. Maybe a hundred things. He turned over and caught his arm in the mosquito netting. He could hear them whining round the room and he remembered something he had been told, that the little devils could fly at the speed of sound, that it was only the females who sucked the blood.

Apt, he thought and closed his eyes, then opened them almost immediately as the door creaked. Someone was in the room. He reached under the net and scrabbled at the bedside table for some kind of weapon, found something and raised it.

'Who is it?' he said, his voice cracking. He felt his heart batter against his ribs and the sweat pump from his forehead, his memory sabotaging him, conjuring up stories of the Mau Mau and dreadful tales of voodoo. 'I warn you,' he said. 'I'm armed.'

The light went on and he groaned with relief. It was only the Governor's ridiculous wife, standing by the door, fingers to her lips for silence. She was wearing some kind of négligé and smelled of drink.

'Mrs Thwaites,' he said sternly, 'what are you doing?'

He glanced down, saw that he had picked up a fly swatter and clumsily dropped it, as she moved to the bed, dropped to her knees and grabbed his hand.

'Your lordsheep,' she whispered, kissing his ring.

'I'm not a peer, yet. A plain Sir Malcolm will suffice.'

'Oh, Sir Malcolm,' she groaned. 'I would rather die than stay here. Pliss, when you leave, tekk me weeth you.'

He tried to draw back but she held his hand tightly as if she were drowning. 'I can cook,' she said, smiling coyly. 'I am steel yong. My body is firm. Look.' And she whipped the hem of the négligé up and over her face. Sir Malcolm grunted and turned away, telling her to pull herself together.'

'I am desperate,' she said, lowering the négligé again.

'It's the heat, woman,' he said. 'I saw this happen in Zimbabwe to Ferdy Cartwright's wife. A cold bath is the answer.'

She shook her head and clambered onto the bed. Cold baths were not her style and, besides, she had noticed something, a reluctant movement on the part of Sir Malcolm, something over which he had no control. It was her ticket out of Cascara, her one opportunity, and she grabbed it hungrily. With both hands . . .

The rum had done for Miguel. He lay comatose on his bunk, the empty bottle on his chest, oblivious to the discordant snores of Delgado and Garfield in the bunk beds a few feet away, so deep in alcoholic slumber that he did not hear the scrabbling at the cell window and hoarse hisses in Spanish.

Again: 'Pssst'.

Then: 'Delgado'.

Delgado woke with a start, sat up and banged his head on the top bunk, then blinked, swung himself to his feet, tottered to the window and looked into a swarthy face. At first he did not recognise it. This time Angola was dry and smiling at him.

'Cuba says: "Cascara, *si*",' he whispered and pointed to

some viscous substance smeared on the wall beneath the window. Delgado poked his head through the bars and blinked at it.

'Plastic explosive,' said Angola. 'I set the timer for five minutes. Take cover, comrade.'

And he was gone. Delgado came instantly awake, leapt back to the bunks and shook Garfield who grunted an obscenity at him.

'We're breaking out of here,' Delgado whispered, slapping his face.

'You spoke,' Garfield whispered back.

'That was only a whisper.'

'You broke your vow.'

'I couldn't find a rhyme for bomb,' he whispered in exasperation.

'Bomb? Whose bomb?'

'The Cubans'.'

'But you made a deal with the British.'

'The Cubans got here first,' Delgado grunted, then pulled the little man by the feet off his bunk and shoved him into the gap beneath the bottom bunk, pulling a mattress over them for protection.

Bloody questions, he thought. We're about to get blown up and he starts an interrogation. Their feet stuck out but there was nothing more he could do. Their feet would have to fend for themselves.

'The Cubans will never get us tickets for Wimbledon,' Garfield grumbled until an elbow in the throat silenced him...

Outside, Angola and Jesus waited, fingers in their ears, crouching behind a wall. Their training had prepared them for this moment. It would be glorious and fulfilling, taking the revolution into the heartland of imperialism. Angola only hoped that he had set the explosives properly. He'd never blown anything up before, not in anger. It was different from the camps where they just played with plasticine. He hoped he'd got the amounts right. If he hadn't, it was too late to do anything about it.

The sound of footsteps on the track from the town made them turn to their right. A vision approached them, carrying a basket. Angola was old enough to remember such women in the old days before they had to wear fatigues and no make-up. Jesus, for his part, had seen *The Hunchback of Notre Dame* in the bad old Batista days and this creature, dressed like a gypsy, could be Esmeralda, if the hair had been dark. She turned and walked to the prison door. This was no vision, thought Angola, this was a problem.

Quickly he leapt over the wall, with Jesus behind him, and scuttled towards her. Pamela saw them and stopped, calmly put down her basket and reached into her handbag.

'I know how to deal with skuzballs like you,' she said. 'I lived in New York for three years.'

She pulled out a gold spray, aimed it at them, pressed the nozzle and smelled scent.

'Oh, my God,' she said as they grabbed her. 'It's my cologne.'

Her head snapped back as Jesus held her from behind, his arm round her throat, and she was staring at the point of a knife.

'One word and you die,' said Angola.

Pamela wasn't having that. She knew about muggers. You had to negotiate with them.

'Who are you?' she whispered.

'That's three words,' said Jesus.

'*Silencio!*' said Angola. 'We are comrades of the Rebel.'

Pamela smiled at the knife and sagged in relief. 'Delgado,' she said. 'He's my friend.'

'*Que?*'

'I'm house-sitting for him. I'm Pamela Weintraub.'

She held out her hand. Angola looked at it for a moment, then shook it.

'What you do here?' Jesus said, reluctantly letting her go. He had been enjoying the body contact.

'Every night I bring him some cooked food,' she explained, pointing to the basket. 'You can imagine how gross prison chow is. Carbohydrate city.' She smoothed her dress and smiled at them. 'What's going down, guys?'

'Jail break,' said Angola. 'Then we move into the hills.'

Pamela squealed with delight. 'Fantastic. I'm coming with you. Do I have time to pack a bag?'

Angola was considering this when he was distracted by the sound of an engine and blinded by headlights. Quickly he pulled Pamela down and dragged her back to the safety of the wall. A Morris Minor stopped in front of the jail and a tall figure got out.

'It's Baxter,' said Pamela.

'The bomb goes off in two minutes,' stated Jesus.

'Bomb?' echoed Pamela, suddenly frightened. 'He'll be killed.'

'Then he will be the first victim of the revolution,' said Angola, grabbing her and pulling her down, his hand over her mouth to keep her quiet.

Baxter had driven all the way round the island trying to control his anger but he had failed. Human nature was a pain in the arse, he had decided. Nobility was dead. There was no such thing as altruism. It was all greed and self-interest and the devil take the hindmost. The phrase conjured up Delgado's face. He looked a bit devilish with the pointed beard and the fierce eyes. Maybe he had cloven hooves. Anyway, Baxter thought, to hell with him. He was disappointed in the man. However misguided Delgado might have been, at least he had had his values and a sense of honour; or so it had seemed until someone came along and offered to buy his soul.

Damn him, he thought, as he parked the car and strode angrily and stuffed with disillusion into the jail, pushed the door open, walked across the room and stared at the inert body of Miguel.

'Good to see security is as tight as ever,' he muttered, then turned and looked at the cell. He was going to wake

102

the bloody Rebel up and give him a piece of his mind. The only problem was: the cell was empty.

'Good God,' he muttered, thinking Sir Malcolm hadn't wasted any time. He grabbed the keys from Miguel's bed and strode to the cell door, then saw the four pink soles under the bunk, two black legs and two white.

'Are you digging a tunnel?' he asked as he unlocked the door. 'Or committing an unnatural act?'

'Go away, Governor,' said Garfield, his voice muffled by the mattress.

'Not till I've had a word with your leader.'

He walked in, leant against the bunks and glared at Delgado's feet.

'I'm disgusted with you, Delgado,' he said. 'No wonder you don't dare show your face.'

'Get out of here,' Delgado said.

Baxter moved to the window and leant against the wall. 'So you're speaking now, are you? I'm not surprised. You've sold out all your other principles.' He sniffed in disgust. 'Whatever our differences, I always thought you and I were the people who cared most about Cascara.'

Delgado scrabbled backwards and turned. On his knees and panting, he reminded Baxter of a rather scabby mongrel.

'I'm begging you on my hands and knees,' Delgado said.

But Baxter wasn't interested. The sight of the man sickened him. He turned away in disgust. 'I've given Cascara jobs and security. All you're going to bring it is chaos, bloodshed and violence.'

He turned back to glimpse a horrifying sight, something out of his nightmares – Delgado rearing up at him, eyes bulging, tongue between his teeth, lunging at him, catching him round his knees and, just as they hit the ground, Baxter's whole world exploded, deafening him, so that all he could remember later was that terrible face and the dreadful fumes of betelwok soup.

Then he was being dragged outside, vaguely aware of

men in combat gear manhandling him, then Pamela's voice asking if he was all right, and a pistol being aimed at him and he thought he was going to die; then a grunt and some Hispanic saying he was worth more alive as a hostage; and then he was being dragged away, into the hills, gagging at the combined stench of Havanas and garlic.

A mile to the west Sir Malcolm had been wakened suddenly from a troubled sleep and sat up trembling. Something had exploded. What on earth was it?

A mumbled response came from the bed. '*Que, mi amor?*'

He closed his eyes and it all came back. He hadn't, had he? Oh yes, he had. Oh Jesus. He remembered it all clearly now, in glorious technicolour and eight-track Dolby sound. He remembered trying to free himself from her clutches, explaining about his wife and children, saying that he could not possibly risk compromising himself, telling her that one whiff of scandal could cause him irreparable damage, yet, even as he had protested, it was already too late; the sheet had been pulled over him and they were actually at it and he remembered saying: 'Actually, I shouldn't even be doing this.'

And now she was lying beside him and the bloody earth was moving.

'How long has that volcano of yours been dormant?' he asked.

She stirred, sat up on one elbow and kissed his shoulder. 'As long. as me,' she said. 'But perhaps you have awakened us both.'

And then he was being grabbed again and forced down, ever downwards.

Thirteen

It was dawn and the bugs were biting, delighted, Baxter thought, to be presented with unexpected breakfast walking right through them in single file up the volcano. It was bad enough for the others but worse for him. With his hands tied he couldn't slap them away. He felt like a horse without a tail.

Baxter was third in the line, Angola leading, Jesus taking the rear, both Cubans stumbling under the weight of their waterproof backpacks. Baxter was wondering what the packs contained, when his thoughts were interrupted by Delgado tapping him on the shoulder and grinning at him.

'This is great, eh Baxter?' he said. 'Plastic bombs. Jailbreaks. A band of desperadoes forging their way through the bush.'

'I suppose I should thank you for saving my life,' he said with little enthusiasm.

'Aye, well,' said Delgado magnanimously. 'Call me a sentimental old fool, but we did once play on the same cricket team.'

At this there was a roar of *'silencio'* from Jesus. 'Don't speak to the prisoner,' he yelled.

'Okay, pal,' Delgado muttered. 'Keep yer hair on.'

Then a complaint from Pamela. 'Did anyone bring any insect repellant? I'm being eaten alive.'

Now it was Angola's turn to call for some discipline. He turned on her and scowled. 'If you are with us, be like our women in Cuba. Fight like a man, think like a man. Already you slow us down.'

'Is it my fault my heel broke?' she yelled back at him, and he grunted a string of Spanish oaths and hacked even harder with his machete.

Baxter, meanwhile, tried to recall his Army training, keeping a memory check on details of the trail, where the sun was and all that, but gave up. Cascara wasn't exactly the Amazon jungle. You couldn't walk far without coming to the other side. If he could manage to escape, he wasn't going to be lost for long.

Baxter guessed that they had been walking for about forty minutes when they came to a clearing and stopped outside a broken-down shack. He turned and could see the port beneath him, then his hands were being untied and he flopped against the shack door, watching as the Cubans began to unload their packs and he could see now why they had seemed so heavy.

First came a Kalashnikov sub-machine gun, then an Armalite rifle followed by a bazooka, a mortar and grenades. He glanced at Pamela, saw her excitement and again he was disappointed. A romantic fool, he thought. He almost wished that she could see one of those dreadful things in action, just to get an idea what they could do to the human body, then maybe she would grow up a little and perhaps cry, and he would maybe take her in his arms and comfort her...

The final package was long and thin. Angola handed it to Delgado with a flourish.

'*Finalmente*,' he said. 'A special gift from Fidel himself.'

Delgado opened it and stepped back, beaming like a kid at Christmas and, when he took out the guitar, he handled it with awe.

'Look at this, Garfield,' he said. 'A stratocruiser.'

Garfield nodded and looked into an accompanying container. 'With two mesa-boogie amps and a ten KPA,' he said.

Baxter was unimpressed. 'Judas sold out for thirty pieces of silver,' he said. 'You've done it for a new sound system.'

Delgado turned and glared at him. 'Get off my case, Baxter. I'm the voice of the people and now they can hear me in stereo.'

Baxter shook his head and turned on Pamela who was vainly trying to start a fire with some twigs and her lighter from Tiffanys.

'And what are you, Pamela? Camp counsellor and revolutionary groupie?'

She pouted at him, stung by his words. 'I can help in lots of ways,' she said indignantly. 'The guys need headlines and I can get them a lot of ink. Just imagine...'

She painted a headline in the air. '"Franklin Spender's daughter joins Rebs." That's page one worldwide.'

The four revolutionaries turned as one and stared at her.

'You are the daughter of Franklin Spender?' Angola asked. 'The Spenco Spender?'

Pamela nodded happily. 'Si, si. Franklin Spender is *mi padre*. Didn't I ever mention it?'

The Cubans went into a huddle, chattering in Spanish, and Pamela turned her smile on Baxter. He shook his head. 'Welcome aboard, Pamela. You've just become their second hostage.'

She spun round again and her smile faded. The Kalashnikov looked different when it was pointing at your head, she thought. Her perception had suddenly altered and Baxter, seeing her face, felt ashamed of himself for being so damned smug...

It took them another twenty minutes to get themselves organised and tie Baxter and Pamela to a coconut tree, then they were off back the way they had come, Delgado carrying the bazooka over his shoulder and giving them a wave and a happy cheerio-then.

Baxter watched them go. They weren't very good

revolutionaries. Good revolutionaries wouldn't have disclosed their plans in front of the hostages. Good revolutionaries would have searched the hostages. It was elementary. Good revolutionaries would have left a guard. It did not need four men to fire one bazooka.

They stood side by side, Pamela to his right, warm and supple against him and indulging in introspection.

'You know, for years I used to agonise over the burning issues of the day. Social injustice, the plight of the Third World, the uneven distribution of wealth. And then I realised. I was doing all my agonising in the Russian Tea Room. So I said: "Pamela, you have got to get involved."'

'Is this involved enough for you?'

But she ignored him. Basically she didn't need an audience. She was talking to herself.

'That explains all my causes and crusades. My analyst says it's a desire to find a meaningful role in life. It's quite a burden to know that you're the seventh ranked heiress in the world.'

'Can you move your left hand at all?'

For a moment she looked surprised to hear his voice, then she wriggled. 'A little,' she said. 'Why?'

'In my pocket you'll find a lighter. We may be able to burn through the ropes.'

She began to reach for him but got waylaid again by her dilemma.

'My only consolation is imagining Dad's face when he hears I'm a hostage. They'd better not ask for less than five mill or he won't even pick up the phone.'

'Pamela,' said Baxter impatiently. 'If you can reach my lighter, Dad may never even get the call.'

The penny dropped. 'Oh. You mean, escape?'

Baxter nodded. 'Unless you'd like another hour of therapy in whch case my fee is fifty dollars.'

She nodded and began to grope harder, asking him to move closer. It was a struggle against the ropes but he managed. Then she smiled. 'I think I've got it, Baxter.'

'No,' he said. 'That's not it.'

'It isn't?' She blushed and stammered an apology.

'Please, don't apologise,' Baxter said in a curiously high-pitched voice. 'But maybe we should find the lighter first.'

And she giggled; like a schoolgirl.

At Government House, Sir Malcolm was busily supervising the fortifications in the event of an attack. As a concession to the heat he had taken off his jacket, but the bowler was firmly in place, a token of his authority; kept the bloody darkies on their toes, he reckoned. He was glad that there was work to be done. Took his mind off his problems. At least the Governor was nowhere to be seen and that was something. He could do without a confrontation with Baxter Thwaites. In a moment of self-awareness he realised that he felt a tremor of guilt. Should have taken his own advice and found a cold shower; except that there was no cold water on the island – what there was dribbled brown and lukewarm out of the taps and swam with cockroaches.

There was no penicillin on the island either, which was a great pity in the circumstances.

A group of men were lazily stacking sandbags around the house and he watched them, his frustration growing. They were so bloody slow. God knows what would happen if they ever discovered trade unions.

It was time, he thought, for a pep talk.

'I want sandbags all round the house,' he roared. 'Every window boarded up and the roof fortified. 'We're dealing with terrorists here. They've already blown up the jail and this house could be their next target.'

Just then a small boy skidded up to him on a bicycle and handed him an envelope.

'What's this, you grubby child?' he said irritably, annoyed at the interruption.

'How about a dollar?' said the kid.

'How about a clip round the ear? Now bugger off.'

He opened the envelope and took out a piece of paper, a

scrawl of block capitals. Pepito joined him, looking over his shoulder, asking what it was.

'It's a sort of ransom note,' he said, squinting. 'They're holding Thwaites and some woman called Weintraub...' he skimmed the rest of it, '... blah, blah, kill the hostages unless their demands are met.'

He looked up and realised that everyone had stopped work to listen.

'Don't stand gawking,' he yelled. 'There's work to be done.'

The only one to continue working uninterrupted was Nado. He was enjoying what he was doing. It hadn't seemed much fun, nailing boards across a bedroom window until he realised which bedroom it was.

The sound of hammering woke Dolores from a slumber and dreams she was ashamed of. She blinked, confused. It was morning but it was growing darker by the minute. Boards were being nailed across the window and she thought she could see through a gap the malevolent features of Nado, his mouth a pincushion of two-inch nails.

She screamed and called for her God. 'They're sealing me in,' she yelled and dashed for the door.

Ken Warden, presenter, anchorman and interviewer with CBS, New York, was flushed with nervous tension, his brain in turmoil ever since the previous evening when he had got the word to get his ass to a place he'd never heard of; but he hadn't complained. This story was a godsend. So far neither NBC nor ABC had shown up, or Channel 7 or anyone. He had the story to himself, just because he had been interviewing an ancient writer on St Lucia; that was the lucky shot, and now he had a two, maybe three hour beat on the others.

He stood on the jetty going over his lines while behind him the crew set up the camera and the sound. He'd already got the ruined jailhouse in the can and now he was just waiting for the interview with what-was-his-name-? Sir Malcolm somebody.

He checked his notes and bit his fingernails. This was the big one. He was already a well-known face coast-to-coast and highly regarded for his tough line of questioning, but it was all indoors – couch work. The men he envied were the war correspondents who could trip Phnom Penh and Saigon off their tongues. They were the heroes, the ones who got the best pussy.

He looked around him. Port Agnes was hardly Saigon but, on the other hand, who had heard of the Falklands before Galtieri, or Grenada before Maurice Bishop?

If he could keep Cascara on the boil, who knows what might be next? El Salvador and Nicaragua were only a short hop away geographically, but a huge leap, career-wise.

'Here he comes,' said his PA and he glanced along the jetty to see Sir Malcolm striding towards him, waving a piece of paper. Ideal, he thought; pin-stripes and an old school tie. A cliché. And clichés, he knew from experience, were good copy, ratings-wise.

Delgado was delirious with excitement. This was what he had dreamed of. This was what it was all about, squatting with his comrades on the hill above the port with a bazooka over his arm. This was history books. Already he could see himself shoulder to shoulder with Gromyko, getting one of those pecks on his cheek.

'Great, eh?' he said to Jesus, but the Cuban wasn't listening. He was watching Angola who was staring through binoculars at the jetty.

'*Perfecto,*' Angola said and handed them to Delgado, then turned to Jesus.

'Tell me the three vital elements we learn at Moscow University for provoking insurgency in undeveloped nations.'

Jesus frowned and shook his head.

'Tit,' said Angola impatiently and Jesus grinned. 'Ah yes, tit. Terror, Infiltration, Television.'

'*Si,*' said Angola.

Delgado lowered the binoculars and nodded. 'American television, Garfield,' he said. 'Just imagine it. The Singing Rebel strikes.'

'Rebels,' said Garfield.

'Yeh. The Singing Rebels strike. Film at Eleven.'

Angola lifted the bazooka onto his shoulder and took aim.

'Coast to coast,' he said...

Everyone was ready. The PA snapped her fingers, Ken Warden turned his profile to the camera and pointed the mike at his interviewee. In the background, in shot, the Union Jack fluttered above the Customs shed.

'Sir Malcolm Leveridge, as spokesman for the British Government, do you feel that the jailbreak and the taking of hostages indicate a growing measure of support for the Cascaran Liberation Movement?'

Sir Malcolm sneered at him and shook his head. 'There is no movement. The only support the Rebel has is a bongo player. This is simply a localised incident which you people, typically, if I may say so, are blowing up out of all proportion.' Sir Malcolm had worked out his strategy. Start the campaign by blaming it on the media. Never failed.

'Under British rule,' he continued, 'this island has always been a model of stability, common sense and tranquilli...'

The last word went unheard as the bazooka shell hit the Customs shed and demolished it. Deafened but exhilarated, terrified but striving to remain a pro – the camera was running after all – Ken Warden hit the jetty on his knees, scooped up some dirt and smeared his face.

The cameraman caught the chaos. The Union Jack toppling, the flames and the smoke, an old man coming out of a little shed buttoning up his trousers, the flames reaching maybe thirty feet. Later he would curse himself for missing the best shot of all; the representative of Her

Majesty's Government belly-flopping off the jetty into the Caribbean and doing a fast Australian crawl in the direction of St Lucia. But he simply never saw it.

Instead, he moved towards the building, keeping the flag in shot, while Ken Warden composed himself, sufficiently to get in front of the shattered building, in close-up, and improvise.

'The Caribbean,' he said solemnly, enunciating carefully. 'Once famous for its blue seas and sunny beaches, and now more noted as a hotbed of political turmoil, today gave us a new name in its catalogue of potential trouble spots.' He paused for exactly three seconds. 'Ken Warden, from Cascara, island in ferment.'

Fourteen

It had taken some time and effort and a few moments of panic when the tree began to smoulder, but they had done it. As Baxter threw off the last strand of rope, they heard an explosion from the port. So, the revolutionaries would be back in about forty minutes. They had enough time to get ready.

Baxter picked up a Kalashnikov and fiddled with it. He'd never handled one of those and he was counting on them not to know or care. It would be a bluff, but bluffs usually worked when a gun was pointing at your groin. Pamela was keeping watch down the trail when he called to her to come back to the tree. She looked at the gun and shuddered.

'Baxter, there are four of them, and they're all armed.'

He nodded. 'That's where you come in. You'll provide a diversion.'

'How?'

'Lie down here,' he pointed to the base of the tree.

'Lie down?'

Now, he thought, came the hard part. Maybe she wouldn't go for it, but he had to try.

'We'll make it look as if I got free and ...' he paused, '... attacked you.'

Her eyes widened, the picture of innocence. 'Why would you do that?'

Baxter looked at the sun and blinked, searching for a way to explain, without offending her sensibilities. 'I might be angry with you for siding with the Rebel ... and the heat might inflame my senses.' He looked directly at her. She was standing, hands on hips in her gypsy dress. 'After all, you're a very attractive woman.'

Pamela smiled and did as she was asked, needing no second bidding. After all, she reminded herself, she'd always been a good actress, at high school and college. They had raved about her Desdemona at Yassar. She'd kept the clipping.

She settled herself against the tree, one arm behind her head and improvised. 'How would I look if I'd been ravished?'

Baxter swallowed hard and shrugged. 'Well,' he said, 'your hair would be ruffled.' He bent towards her and ruffled her hair. It felt like silk. Images of a pillow raced across his brain.

'And I think this button undone...' He carefully undid the top button, took a deep breath and went further down, '... and maybe this one.'

She smiled at him, thinking herself into the part, looking down at herself.

'Oh, I think you'd have ripped off my sleeve,' she said and drew her arm out of her right sleeve, exposing her shoulder and a lot of breast.

She looked at him closely, thinking he would make a wonderful Othello. He seemed to be thinking himself into the part also. He had gone slightly red in the face.

'You'd have been surprised by the intensity of your passion,' she said, thinking of her Stanislavsky class on motivation. 'You would have been overcome by an insatiable hunger and lust for me.'

He came closer and, as he reached for her, she thought that he would make some actor, for he sure as dammit was simulating lust pretty well.

They kissed, rehearsing their roles. She closed her eyes and thought of Othello. The rehearsal seemed to last for an eternity and, when it was over, she was breathless.

'You once called me an undesirable alien,' she said.
'I lied.'

And the rehearsals began again.

The revolutionaries were in high spirits as they made
their way back up the trail – Angola, as ever, in the lead,
Delgado in charge of the bazooka. It was warm, whether
from the firing or the sun he did not know. And he could
smell sulphur, although that might have been the
volcano; but he wasn't about to split hairs, not with the
revolution under way. Two explosions in a matter of
hours. The tinder box had been ignited and now surely all
the Caribbean still under imperialist rule would burn.

As they reached the clearing, Angola held up his hand
for silence. They grouped around him, wondering why
they had stopped, then followed his gaze and saw Pamela
lying stretched out by the tree, her eyes closed. They
blinked at the sight of so much exposed flesh and a
communal groan escaped from them as they ran towards
her, Angola and Jesus arguing fiercely. 'You tied the
knots.' 'No, I didn't, I just held my finger on the rope and
you tied them.' 'No, I didn't, you did.'

'Didn't.'

'Did.'

'Didn't.'

'Did...'

And all in Spanish, but Delgado knew enough to realise
that something was terribly wrong.

As they reached her, she opened one eye and smiled at
them, then from behind came a familiar voice.

'All right, let's have no martyrs for the revolution.'
They turned. Baxter stood on the rise some ten feet away,
the Kalashnikov held hip high, as if he knew what he was
doing. 'Drop your guns,' he said, 'put your hands behind
your heads, and Pamela, button your blouse.'

They all did as they were told, Pamela surprising
herself. She'd never enjoyed being ordered around by a
man before.

Delgado had never known such misery. One moment he
was delirious with happiness, the next, disarmed and

116

disgusted with himself. Baxter was leading the way along
the river. It stank of sulphur and buzzed with flies and
Delgado didn't even bother slapping at the bites. Jaws on
wings, millions of them, but he didn't care. For a while, on
the march south, he thought about jumping Baxter but
the woman was bringing up the rear and she had the sub-
machinegun. If she decided to open up, it would be sheer
bloody murder and there was something degrading about
being shot by a woman.

At the river bank Baxter turned and held up his hand.
They stood still, waiting, the Cubans terrified, thinking
they were going to be executed; and what a stinking place
to die.

'Okay,' said Baxter, pointing his gun at them, then
waving it to the south. 'Follow the river, watch out for the
mangrove swamp and with luck you'll make Calamity
Cove by nightfall. If your boat is still there, you can set
sail for Havana.'

'And face Fidel after this fiasco?' said Angola. 'No. We
make for Miami. I have a cousin there.'

'Ah, *si*,' said Jesus, smiling with relief that they were to
be spared. 'We go underground and spread sedition.'

'No,' said Angola again, shaking his head. He'd had
enough of revolution. 'We deal coke.'

And they were off, arguing with one another, discussing their failure in Spanish obscenities.

'Can we go with them, Governor?' Garfield asked, but it
was Delgado who replied.

'No, Garfield. It's jail for us. The real thing this time.
Bread and water and solitary.' Already the optimist in
him was thinking ahead. 'I shall write a book. Delgado
Fitzhugh. Volume One. My Years of Struggle.'

'The struggle isn't over,' said Baxter, and Delgado
stared at him in surprise, then ducked as Baxter tossed a
rifle to him.

'Whose side are you on?' he asked, clumsily catching it
and fumbling with the trigger.

'Cascara's,' said Baxter. 'This is my home. And if we

117

don't move fast, we're going to lose it, either to the Cubans or the Brits, or the next bunch who want their grubby paws on it. The only people who can stop that are us.'

Pamela's eyes shone with admiration. 'We're with you all the way,' she said, then turned to Delgado and Garfield. 'Aren't we, guys?'

'But there's only four of us,' Delgado protested. 'And she's a woman.'

Pamela raised her eyes to the sky. 'I can't believe I'm hearing this in the eighties,' she said.

Then they were on the move again, heading west, back towards Port Agnes, Delgado shaking his head in bewilderment. It was all getting to be too much for him.

Ken Warden had found an ideal spot. The early film was on its way to St Thomas and with luck would make the one o'clock news. Safe in the knowledge that he had beaten everyone else, Ken was happy, but there was to be no resting on laurels. The others were on their way. It was time to consolidate.

What he needed was height so that he could be filmed against a background of bush, then the camera would pan left to show the shoreline below and then the horizon, to let the subliminal thought sink into the viewer's brain; the domino theory – first Cascara, then St John and St Thomas, then, he hoped, subconsciously they would connect... next Miami!

Art was what Ken was after now, something more than a mere news report. He wanted something that would stimulate ideas, something that would get him an Emmy.

They were ready for him. He set his features into an expression of deep concern and began:

'Here in Cascara the man they call the Singing Rebel is still at liberty. Together with his two hostages, he has gone underground.'

Behind him Baxter, Delgado, Pamela and Garfield emerged from the bush as he continued. 'And in this remote and inhospitable terrain, he could be in one of a thousand places. Somewhere out there...' He stopped and squinted at his crew, exasperated with them. 'Why do you have your hands in the air, guys? Are we still rolling?'

The answer appeared in his ear, the barrel of the Kalashnikov and a cultured English voice saying: 'The search is over, Ken.'

It had taken almost half a bottle of brandy to steady Sir Malcolm Leveridge's nerves but at last he had stopped trembling. He sat on the Governor's bed next to the Governor's wife and wondered how he would claim his suit on expenses. The salt water had ruined it. But it wasn't a problem. There in fact was no problem. He had just been onto London and the word was good. Now he was trying to explain to Dolores, who was relaxing in a silk slip and silk stockings, cradling a fifth of tequila.

'Between ourselves,' he said, 'London's delighted to have guerrillas creating havoc in the hills. They think I engineered the whole thing. So I'm smelling of roses.'

Dolores smiled at him and tickled him with her toes.

'Of course for you, my dear,' he continued, 'with your husband captive, this is a time of great emotional stress.'

She nodded. 'But you know, my life too could be in danger. Maybe I should be somewhere else...' She thought for a moment, '... like the Riviera?'

'Rather you didn't,' said Sir Malcolm sternly. 'It will look better in the Press if you stay. The loyal little wife bravely choking back a tear. Quivering upper lip, that sort of thing.'

Dolores sighed. 'I suppose I must do my duty.'

'That's the spirit.' He looked at her, the breasts spilling out of the silk and he had an idea. 'Now why don't you slip into that nun's habit again?'

She laughed, kissed him and swung herself off the bed. In for a penny, in for a pound, he thought. Might as well be hung for a sheep as a lamb; then his mind came up with a treacherous piece of word-association. A sheep for a lamb became mutton dressed as lamb. He smiled and decided to

119

lie back and think of England. In moments of extremis, he found himself thinking of Sarah, but what was frightening was that on two occasions he had actually conjured up an image of the PM wielding a whip. It was a dreadful thought, blasphemous even and probably illegal.

Fifteen

Rob Waring wasn't exactly relishing the idea of talking to Franklin Spender but he realised that he had no choice. The news had to come first-hand. He couldn't wait for the man to hear it on television.

The reaction was predictable and very, very loud, Spender's voice booming out of the telephone and echoing around the site office. Waring held it away from his head; being a Spenco executive didn't mean you had to get your goddamn eardrums busted.

'Waring, we're about to launch a multi-million dollar campaign and I'm not going to let some half-baked bunch of Commie revolutionaries foul it up.'

Thought as much, said Waring to himself.

'Now, you've got some good ol' boys down there who must be itchin' to kick some ass,' Spender roared. 'So turn 'em loose and I guarantee they'll blast the shit out of these rebs.'

'Sir,' said Waring, leaping quickly into a pause, 'that might put the hostages in jeopardy.'

'Screw the hostages.'

'That would be the preferred option, sir, but . . .' he took a breath, 'one of them is your daughter.'

There was a moment of silence. Rob counted to five, then: 'We were never that close,' said Spender. And the line went dead.

Slowly he wandered out of the office and down towards the gate in time to see a Toyota Landcruiser come down the track and pull up at the gate. The television logo on the doors brought a group of roughnecks at a run, with Ben in the lead. As Rob approached, he saw Ben look in and heard him squeal. 'Hey, it's Ken Warden. You want to do a piece on us?'

He could see Warden's face, saw him nod, then the gate was opened and the Toyota sped through, Ben running behind it, shouting at it, asking if he had time to trim his beard.

Rob stepped forward, ready to greet them. He was apprehensive. The media could be trouble and he hadn't yet worked out his strategy. It was too early to float the news of the strike, might pre-empt the advertising campaign, and how was he going to handle the problem of Pamela as hostage?

He fixed his smile in place as the Toyota stopped by the rig, then he froze as the rear doors opened and three men jumped out, each one armed to the teeth, bandoleers, machine guns and God knows what. What the hell was the Governor doing dressed up like Che Guevara? Why was the little black guy trussed up with sticks of dynamite? And what the hell was Pamela doing pointing a gun at him?

Even as his brain went into spasm, the others were reacting, reaching for hammers and pieces of pipe and moving towards the little group. Then Baxter picked up a bullhorn marked CBS and yelled: 'Hold it! One move and we explode the well.'

He raised a grenade, the men stopped in their tracks and Delgado burst into song:

'All you sons of
Imperial-is-um...'

'Skip the song, Delgado,' Baxter muttered. 'Just tell them we're desperate and we'll die for the cause.'

As Delgado told them, Baxter took out his lighter and held it an inch from Garfield's body. At first it wouldn't light. He cursed and flicked it until a small flame appeared. The gelignite began to sweat and so did Garfield.

Then Rob made another executive decision. 'Do as they say,' he said. And Garfield fainted.

In Houston the game was in its fourth quarter and the Oilers were in trouble. High above the field in his private box, Franklin Spender watched dejectedly through the triple-glazed bullet-proof glass, occasionally checking the plays on the bank of TV screens above his head, and listening to the roars of the crowd, through stereo speakers set in the ceiling.

As always when the Oilers were at home, he invited a few old boys for some beers and some steaks, and for three hours he put the stresses of business life behind him. For those three hours he relaxed, totally and completely. It was one of his strengths, he had always said, to be able to relax for three hours every other Sunday during the football season. Other people had their hobbies. Others took holidays, but Spender had his three hours, and nothing, but nothing, was allowed to interrupt. The only thing was, he could relax better if the damned team were winning.

Now it was crucial. The commentator's voice confirmed what was happening two hundred feet below: it was third and thirteen and the quarterback had to go to the air.

A telephone receiver was flashing but he ignored it, unaware of his secretary's decision to interrupt him. She had agonised over the news for over two hours now and finally made her decision. She could only hope it was the right one.

A hostess dressed in Annie Oakley outfit with short skirt and stetson tugged his arm, held out the phone and whispered:

'It's your daughter calling, Mr Spender.'

He swore at her and took the receiver. Eyes still fixed on the game, he grunted: 'Pamela, this had better be good. We're deep in the fourth quarter and trailing by seven.'

'I'm sorry if this is a bad time, father...' Her voice was a barely audible squeak over the radio phone.

'You know your problem, don't you,' he said, taking time off to lecture her. The Oilers were in a huddle and he had a few seconds. 'You never learned to accept being rich. All you ever did was run around tryin' to screw it up for the rest of us, and look where it's got you. You're probably bein' raped and tortured by a bunch of bandits in a mud hut when all that's mine could have been yours.'

'I now have part of it, Dad.'

He closed his eyes for a moment and missed the play, heard a groan from the others. 'Just a minute, Pamela,' he said and turned. 'What is it?'

'Interception,' said ol' Joe.

'Jesus Christ,' he yelled, glaring at the field. 'That turkey couldn't throw a Hallowe'en party.' He was mad as hell by the time he got back to his daughter and asked her what she was saying.

The reply came back in an exaggerated Texan drawl. 'I said, I have your water, Daddy. And if you don't make a few calls to your friends in high places, I'm going to blow it off the face of the goddamn earth.'

And she hung up. He looked stupidly at the receiver. No one hung up on him, ever. He hit the button, told the operator to get him Waring, drummed his fingers until the call came through and it was confirmed. The rig was wired with gelignite and dynamite and his daughter had the detonator.

'Two billion barrels a year,' he whispered to himself as he wandered out of the room. The others watched him go. Must be ill, they thought, for there were still six minutes eighteen left on the clock.

At the rig, Baxter sat in the dirt, his gun on his knees, contemplating the immediate future. There was enough food to last for days; that was no problem. Oilmen ate like horses and he had seen the supplies. He also knew the psychological pressures that might be brought to bear on him and he looked forward to fighting them. After all, he was well prepared. Like every other ambassador on the

124

planet he had read up on the conditions of siege and he knew what they would be thinking. Gamekeeper turned poacher, he said to himself and smiled.

It was all going to plan. All he wanted was an audience, the chance to put Cascara's case before world opinion. It wasn't much of an ambition but it was enough for him. There would be complicity and duplicity, of that he was sure, but as long as the case was put across, then he had done his job. He had burned his diplomatic boats and his future was uncertain, but he did not care. He hadn't felt so alive since he was in his teens.

Garfield winked at him and he winked back. Pamela smiled and outshone the sun, then a murmur from the roughnecks made him look up the track to see the old Morris Minor bouncing towards them. It stopped at the gates and Pepito heaved himself out followed by Miguel and the two policemen. He got to his feet and walked to the gate, smiled at Pepito. Pepito did not smile back. Instead he drew himself to his full height and, when he spoke, it was in his most formal tone, as if he were opening a session of Parliament.

'As a paid official of Her Majesty's Government, it is my duty to point out that your actions are a flagrant breach of international law.'

Baxter smiled. 'That had occurred to me, Pepito,' he said, hoping that the man wasn't going through one of those 'power corrupts' phases.

'As your adviser,' Pepito continued, ignoring the interruption, 'I should warn you that you will probably be charged with sedition, terrorism, trespass and possibly treason.'

Miguel nodded in agreement. 'You in deep shit, boss,' he said.

'That had occurred to me too,' said Baxter.

Pepito's expression remained officious. 'As your friend I ask ... are you prepared to go through with this?'

'All the way.'

'Then you leave us no choice,' he said and beamed

happily. 'Unlock the gate and we'll join you.'

Baxter grinned and, behind him, Delgado and Garfield whooped with delight. Baxter unlocked the gate and grabbed Pepito by the arm, thanking him, then Miguel and the policemen.

'Now all we have to do is withstand the combined might of Britain and America,' he said.

Arm-in-arm Baxter and Pepito walked back to the rig followed by the others. Now they were eight, Baxter thought; one more than the magnificent seven.

In the Oval Office on 1600 Pennsylvania Avenue, Washington, the military grouped around the President's desk, gazing past him into the rose garden as many had done before them in times of crisis. Adrenalin flowed through thickening arteries as each man tried to put his point of view. The Admiral had the loudest voice and, consequently, for the moment was the most influential.

'Here's an opportunity to show Castro in his own backyard,' he roared, then stepped back as a four-star General took over. 'We send in the Marines,' the old man said, puffing out a scrawny chest, 'like we did in Grenada.'

There was a silence, then one of the Presidential advisers stepped forward. 'It seems to be unanimous, Mister President.'

Another silence. The adviser felt uncomfortable. It wasn't his place after all to take on such responsibility, unilaterally as it were. He looked at the others for support before asking the question.

'Should I wake him?'

In Downing Street, the BBC had been summoned to convey the Prime Minister's message to the nation. She was in her best blue, the hair newly permed, chin held high, the voice unmistakably Churchillian, so much so that the cameraman, in a moment of treacherous irreverence, was reminded of a man called Mike Yarwood.

126

'The British people,' she said, 'will never bow to the tactics of terrorism. The Special Air Service has already been despatched, willing to demonstrate once again the gratuitous violence and mayhem for which they are rightly famous.'

There was no dissent in the country, or none that made itself known and she was reminded, as she would say later, of that marvellous Saturday morning in the spring of eighty-two when no one objected to the great adventure in the South Atlantic.

Decisions had been made and put into operation. The Special Relationship was cemented. The *Hermes* made a U-turn in the Caribbean and, in the dead of night, the Marines prepared to go in.

In Washington and London, men and women at the centre of power held their breaths. Cascara was a boil about to be lanced. The Free World had set out to defend itself from sedition.

Sixteen

For a brief moment, as the sun rose, Jay Jay had thought of taking the day off and joining the others down by the rig. He had asked himself what on earth was the point of playing music to an empty town, to a few dogs and chickens. Not even the old man on the jetty was around to listen to him; but he resisted the idea. He was, after all, a professional, and he liked to hear the music throbbing back at him from below. None of them had turned off their radios when they left. It would have been too much bother; they would only have to turn them on again when they came back.

And so he carried on as if nothing had happened, aware of the fact that he had never cared too much if people listened or not. He played the music for himself anyway. Plus, he would tape his news broadcasts for posterity – if anyone ever wanted to hear the history of Cascara, it would all be on tape.

Hot and windy once more was the weather forecast. He picked up his binoculars and scanned the town. Soon the soldiers would be coming. He had been well warned.

Then he saw them, a line of Marines moving cautiously through a side street towards the square. As they reached it, they took up positions while a sergeant approached a half-open door, his rifle in the ready position.

Jay Jay bent to the mike. 'Welcome to the Eighty-Second Airborne,' he said and the sergeant spun around, startled. 'Radio Moscow just described your presence here as an act of provocation, detrimental to world peace.'

For a moment the sergeant froze, then rushed at the door of the house and kicked it open, staggering back under the assault of two chickens and a kitten.

'Hey, man,' said Jay Jay, 'don't kick our doors down. You won't find nobody. They're all at the well.' He grinned into the mike. 'Why don't you head on over? They got barbecued goat, pretty girls and dancing till midnight with T-Bone Jefferson and his steel band.'

He was about to turn and view the reaction when there was a terrible, and now familiar, splintering sound. Jay Jay groaned as another body hurtled through his roof trailing parachute lines. From the oaths Jay Jay made a calculated guess as he leant once more into the mike.

'Meanwhile, Britain has begun its own military build-up on the island...'

It was fiesta time on the hillside outside the Spenco fence. It was Mardi Gras and Carnival, the biggest jump-up in living memory, and T-Bone was making the most of it. For once he had no competition from Jay Jay and his taped music. And besides, there was a semi-circle of cameras pointed at him. The world's Press was there. They had been arriving by helicopter and launch, and now every major network was represented along with the scribblers from the newspapers and a scrum of photographers. It was too good for T-Bone to miss. He grinned and waved as he sang, thinking of fame and fortune and an opportunity that came once in a lifetime.

The women danced. The men smoke, drank and told each other lies. The kids played cricket. They'd chalked a set of stumps on the Spenco gate and were happily on their eighth innings.

Only Ah Fong was working. He had been up all night with his stencil set and now he was selling the fruits of his labours, T-shirts of the Rebel stencilled over the map of Cascara; small, medium, large and extra large.

Every so often, a runner from the news groups would

approach the gate and offer money for exclusives, but there were no takers. The roughnecks had been permitted to leave and only Rob Waring and Ben remained at their posts.

The hillside throbbed to a babble of languages as French, German and Japanese told the story of Cascara to the viewers back home while the newspapermen grumbled about lack of telephones.

'Here on Cascara,' said the man from the BBC, 'tension is rising. We have just heard that renegade Governor, Baxter Thwaites, has called for a confrontation with the British authorities in order to issue his demands. And, as the carnival atmosphere indicates, this is not an isolated act by a fanatical majority, but a movement which has won the hearts and minds of the people.'

Next to him, an American reporter had a different angle: 'Once again,' she said dramatically, 'American soldiers have set foot on foreign soil in a land that last week they had never heard of. And many of them are searching their hearts and saying: "Why are we here?"'

A young Marine overheard her and thought it was a good question. He turned and put it to his Major who was impatiently surveying the scene.

'Why are we here?' growled the Major. 'Because we're a friggin' peace-keeping corps. Which means we can't squeeze a trigger until those wise-ass pinko media personnel have shipped outta here.'

The Marine nodded, satisfied, then turned as a jeep appeared on the brow of the hill, filled with British paratroops. Their leader vaulted out and trotted towards them, nodded a greeting at his American counterpart and introduced himself.

'We have to move these civilians,' said the American. 'Can't see the target for limbo dancers.'

'But these are innocent bystanders,' replied the Englishman.

'There's no such thing in my experience. They're all hand in glove with the gooks.'

'We're not in Vietnam now, Major,' said the Englishman reprovingly. 'Those chaps carry British passports. And if any of them have to die, it will be by a British bullet.'

The two allies glared at each other, each one fingering his weapon. It was a stalemate, a stand-off which might have become nasty if they hadn't been diverted by the sound of a motor horn blaring. Fifty lenses turned as one towards a British Army Land Rover rattling towards them over the brow of the hill, the lenses catching the sun and blinding the driver so that he skidded to a halt, almost overturning the vehicle. Sir Malcolm was the first to get out, leaving Eric NcNab in the back wedged between Dolores and a very fat black woman with greying hair.

There was a moment of silence, except for the whirr of mótorised cameras harmonising with the clicking of the cicadas, then a murmur of questions in ten languages as the reporters asked each other who the people were with the man from Whitehall.

Sir Malcolm picked up a loudhailer from the Land Rover and handed it to Eric, whispering to him to do his best. The old man lurched to his feet and helped the fat woman up, put his arm round her shoulder and hoisted the hailer.

'Delgado,' he shouted. 'Your mother and I are both here.'

The cameras went mad and in the compound Delgado dropped to his knees, his howl of 'Aw nawww', clearly audible.

Sir Malcolm, watching the compound, saw an extraordinarily beautiful young woman lean over Delgado's shoulder to comfort him and idly wondered what she might look like in a traffic warden's uniform.

'We're both appealing to you,' Eric shouted, his voice echoing around the bay. 'Lay down your arms.'

Delgado buried his face in his hands as the TV cameras turned on him, but it was Baxter who took up the response. He walked towards the gate and shouted: 'It's too late for that, Eric.'

Sir Malcolm swore beneath his breath at the sight of the man. He was a disgrace to the Diplomatic Corps, dressed in khaki like some overgrown Boy Scout. Impatiently he grabbed the hailer from Eric and roared into it:

'Thwaites, I don't know what you hope to achieve, but before you do anything rash, I'd like to remind you of your duties to the Crown. And, of course, your responsibilities to Dolores, your distraught wife of fourteen years.'

Dolores got to her feet and waved her regal wave. She had dressed for the occasion, a summer frock and matching hat, as if she were going to open a village fete in Sussex. Baxter ignored her and addressed himself to Sir Malcolm.

'I know my responsibilities,' he said, then turned to Garfield, who stood at the gate, and told him to open it and let Sir Malcolm through.

As Sir Malcolm made his way down the track, Baxter walked forward to meet him, thumbs in his bandoleer, then stopped, legs apart, inside the gate, on his own ground.

Sir Malcolm was halfway down the slope when the English Major caught up with him and whispered in his ear. 'Don't worry, sir. I've got a sniper positioned. One nod from you and he'll shoot the bastard's pecker off.'

Sir Malcolm shuddered slightly. 'Thank you, Major,' he said, 'but I'm sure diplomacy will prevail.'

Then he was on his own, the might of the military behind him, ready to do what he was good at, to negotiate with idiots. He ignored Garfield at the gate and sauntered up to Baxter, stopped and shook his head.

'What do you look like, Thwaites? You haven't shaved, you smell like a rancid goat and you've thrown in your lot with a bunch of grubby guerrillas.' He tutted and sighed. 'You've become the Patty Hearst of the British Diplomatic Corps.'

Baxter smiled at him, affecting innocence. 'I'm just

helping to foment revolution,' he said. 'Wasn't that the British plan in the first place?'

It was. Sir Malcolm could see grounds for optimism, 'I see ... well, you have rather exceeded your brief, but my deal with Delgado still holds, does it?'

Baxter shook his head. 'All deals are off.' And he put his idea, the idea that had come to him as he had surveyed the ranks of the world's Press and Pamela had mentioned something about a United Nations of media folk. 'You and the Americans have to agree to let the Rebel appear before the United Nations to put the case for Cascaran independence. We shall abide by their vote.'

Sir Malcolm was appalled. He'd never heard such nonsense. 'You can't do this,' he spluttered. 'Think of England. Think of Duty. Think of Me.'

'We'll deal with you just like anybody else,' said Baxter patiently. 'I expect some of the water will trickle your way.'

Sir Malcolm opened his mouth to argue, then stood stock still at the sound of a familiar voice roaring through the loudhailer – the voice of his nightmares. He couldn't bring himself to turn and look at it.

'Have you tole heem about us, Malcolm,' Dolores yelled and again the cameras swivelled as one.

'Eeet ees true, Baxter,' she shouted. 'We were powerless to reseest. I want a divorce so that Sir Malcolm and I can be married.'

The crowd cheered. Baxter grinned and Sir Malcolm spun round, apoplectic, seeping tension, searching for help.

'Shut that woman up, Major,' he shouted. 'Where's your bloody sniper, man?' Meanwhile behind him, Baxter offered his congratulations and the hope that they would both be very happy.

The same group had convened once more in the White House and now they were angry. As American military men, they abhorred vacillation. It was anathema. It was

133

un-American to haggle. That was the tone of the argument. Far better to get on with things; that was the American way. That was what the President was known for. The trouble was, the Navy was acting wet.

'World opinion is behind them,' the Admiral pointed out. 'The British have agreed. I think we have to play along.'

The four-star General shook with fury at this. 'Just because Thatcher's caved in,' he said, 'do we let these guerrillas squeeeze our prunes? I say we call their bluff.'

At this there was a grunt of 'excuse me' and Franklin Spender stepped into the forefront of the argument. This was the rogue card, talking directly into the face of his President.

'Sir, may I point out that the guerrilla with the finger on the button is my daughter. And I know Pamela. Her favourite pastime ain't the seals, or the whales, or the Navajos; it's shafting dear old Dad.'

The inference was obvious even to a man half-asleep. The rebels wanted to put their case before the UN. Okay, so let them. It would do no harm to appear magnanimous. They would try the peaceful way for a change, and besides, Spenco was one of the single greatest contributors to the Republican Party funds. He nodded agreement and the jaw of the General dropped.

They didn't believe it at the rig until the chopper landed and then they believed. It had UN on the side. It was going to happen. Baxter suspected a trap. He had grown sceptical over the last few days, but he put his scepticism aside and stood back as Delgado and Garfield came out of one of the trailers carrying a spare set of fatigues in polythene wrappings. Ah Fong had anticipated events and had their clothes dry-cleaned. For free. The usual maxim of 'no ticket, no laundry' was suspended, he had said, but make sure to mention my name on First Avenue.

As they made their way towards the chopper, the Cascarans cheered.

'Knock 'em dead, fellas,' said Baxter.

'Bring us independence,' said Pepito.

'Bring me a Yankee baseball jacket,' yelled Miguel from the platform.

And Pamela fussed around them with last-minute instructions. 'Don't come on too strong to begin with,' she said to Delgado, 'Then build! And remember, it's the eyes. The fire, the passion, the feeling, it's all in the eyes.'

He nodded and climbed into the chopper behind Garfield and, as it rose, she yelled after them: 'And you got a great ass, Delgado. Don't be afraid to move it.'

And then they were gone and Baxter's arm was round Pamela's waist, protectively.

As the helicopter headed north, the pilot looked down and blinked, thinking he could see, on an uninhabited island, no more than a piece of volcanic rock, a group of people moving down a cliff face on ropes. There was a word for it. He searched his memory. *Abseiling*. That was it. But it couldn't be. Why on earth would anyone be abseiling in the middle of the Caribbean? He shrugged and turned to check out his passengers. They were both being sick. First-time fliers, he thought. A shame...

Four hundred feet below, Hugo Kessler automatically dropped into the freeze position as the chopper flew over him, and it wasn't until it was out of sight that he turned and watched his men coming down the cliff. As they reached the bottom and ran towards him, he checked his stop-watch. They were fast. Good men. Months of inactivity had done nothing to slow up their reflexes.

Panting, the six men threw themselves into two rubber motor launches and looked at him for approval. They were dressed identically in black combat suits. Each man bore the stamp of his profession somewhere. If it wasn't a smashed nose, it was a scarred cheek. If it was neither, it was a stitched-up bullet wound somewhere beneath the suit. Kessler knew. He knew all of them, from way back.

'Four minutes and sixteen seconds,' he said, then

135

turned to confront the banker. 'Then they rendezvous with the yacht and we are back in Martinique before dawn.'

'Good,' said the banker. She was elegant and forty, the product of the Sorbonne and finishing school in Switzerland, and spoke English with hardly a trace of French accent. 'I congratulate you, Mister Kessler. You have done well.'

Kessler clicked his heels. 'Hand-picked mercenaries, Madame. The scum of the earth.'

'Let me talk to them.'

He nodded and turned to his men, beckoning them forward with roars of '*Achtung, schnell*'. They grouped round her, looking up from the kneeling position, as eager as puppies.

'Gentlemen,' said the banker. 'I can now reveal the purpose of your mission.' They nodded as one. 'French mineral water is the finest in the world, but it is threatened by the upstarts of Cascara. You will destroy their well.'

They murmured to one another in a variety of languages until Kessler held his hand up for silence.

'It is a dangerous mission,' she continued, 'and some of you will die. But remember. In a world gone mad, you will die for the principle that you all hold close to your hearts.' She paused. 'Money.'

They saluted her and yelled back, *Vive le franc! Vive le dollar! Vive le deutschmark!* with Kessler roaring to himself, *Vive le numbered bank account in Zurich*. Then the banker was helped into a power boat which took her away into the anonymity of the ocean.

Kessler watched her go, then turned to his men and outlined the plan of campaign.

That done and understood, he snapped his fingers at the biggest of his men.

'Pierre,' he said, 'tell us about the emergency rations.'

Pierre doubled as the explosives expert and cook and took both professions seriously, aware of the dictum of an army marching on its stomach. The emergency special, he told them, was *carré d'agneau avec flageolets*, followed by green salad and cheese, then *fraises du bois*, accompanied by a robust young St Emilion which would refresh even the most jaded palate.

And the mercenaries licked their lips.

Seventeen

Delgado was in a dream world. First a helicopter, then an exectuive jet with the vastness of the eastern seaboard of America beneath them, then the Jumbo from Miami, then the sight of Manhattan. It was a succession of un-believable images. Then Kennedy Airport and all those people in one place and strange phrases and questions; a succession of images that they couldn't grasp and Garfield saying it was just like the movies and Delgado knowing that the little man had never seen a movie.

Then there was something called a limo to take them along something called the Van Wyck Expressway through something called Queens underneath a minute of blackness called the Holland Tunnel. It was all too much for him. Delgado closed his eyes and when he was prodded out of the limo he was in an underground garage with numbers on the walls, heading for a bank of elevators, with Garfield holding his hand tightly, like a baby; then going up in something called an elevator, ears popping, then coming out into the most amazing room he had ever seen; huge with what they told him was a podium and a great bank of seats reaching way up to a roof as high as the oil rig.

He blinked at the bank of amplifiers being built on both sides of the podium, by men with satin jackets with his face on the back and the words:

Singing Rebel
New York
1985.

It was all too much to take in, with people talking about acoustics and he never having sung indoors in his life. And then they were telling him there was an hour to go ...

It was a full house. No abstentions. The idea had caught on and the delegates took their seats ahead of time. Curiosity, it seemed, was a phenomenon that united them all. No one had ever sung in the UN.

Two floors below the Council Chamber, the director checked his monitors, slapped his hands together and turned to his crew as his PA told him there were thirty seconds to go.

'Paul,' he snapped into the mike, 'I need Russia, so widen the shot. When the Rebels come on, I need Russia's reaction.' His eyes flickered and showed irritation. 'Dave,' he barked out. 'Why are you on Sweden? They wouldn't react if the roof fell in. Find me China or somebody.'

'Twenty seconds,' said the PA.

'Listen, if we need a filler, cut to the map. Let's remind people where this place is.'

'Fifteen seconds.'

'Okay, good luck everybody.' He adjusted his cans. 'Don't forget the world is taking this. This is bigger than the moon walk. We're thinking Emmys here.'

The crew shook hands quickly and bent to their work. The lights dimmed and, on the platform behind the amplifiers, the delegate from Malaya made the announcement:

'Mr Secretary General, honourable ambassadors, please welcome the delegates for the Cascara Liberation Front.'

A spotlight picked out Delgado and Garfield slowly walking towards the podium from the left. Delgado was holding onto his stratocruiser as if it were a life-raft. He had a harmonica fixed at his throat and he was licking his lips, white-faced and nervous. Behind him Garfield rolled his eyes and fiddled with his keyboard. In his control booth the director was reminded of an old vaudeville act, something out of the Black and White

139

Minstrels. There was a short shower of applause as they reached centre stage and peered at their audience. Delgado took a deep breath. It was the moment he had dreamed of, actually playing indoors for the first time in his life.

Garfield was looking at him, waiting for his cue. Delgado nodded, tapped one foot and hit a C chord. It sounded tinny but it was all he had.

Then he sang, softly and earnestly as Pamela had told him: 'Don't come on strong to begin with...'

'Out of Africa and Europe across many oceans
We came to Cascara,
The stars and the fates
Brought us to Cascara's land
And brother to brother, sister to sister
As one people we stand...'

The camera panned around the hall showing boredom, and the director groaned. He was no student of music but he knew the diference between good television and bad.

'Is this dull?' he asked his PA.

'This is dull,' she said.

'Unless that guitar's a machine gun, we're in trouble,' he said, suddenly wishing he were somewhere else, like an outside broadcast from Buffalo...

On the island, the fiesta was adjourned for the moment and the Cascarans stood silently in groups listening to the broadcast relayed through loudspeakers. In the site office Baxter and Pamela watched a small portable TV. Behind them, Pepito and Miguel were half-heartedly snapping their fingers, trying to find the rhythm.

'And the lands of our ancestors
Are centuries away...'

'If independence depends on this song,' Baxter said, 'we may as well give the island back to the bats.'

'It gets better,' said Pamela, smiling at the screen.

'How do you know?'

'I have a lot of friends in the music business. I made a few calls.'

Delgado was coming to the end of the first verse.

'So give us our home
Give us our nation today.'

A pause, a beat of silence, then he raised his arm and hit a chord: 'TODAY!' he sang and on cue a great wave of sound, a surge-tide of rhythm broke over the audience and the lights came up to show a group of musicians arranged behind Delgado and Garfield.

The director jumped to his feet and pointed at the monitor; at a small greying drummer hammering the skins.

'That's Ringo whosits,' he stammered.

'Starr,' said his PA.

'And George whatsits...'

'Harrison.'

'Whosits and whatsits,' he burbled, 'together again.'

The PA was a music lover and she filled him in on the names as he directed his cameras.

'That's Ray Cooper playing drums next to Ringo, John Lord on guitar, Mike Moran on keyboard and Chris Stainton...'

'And that's Eric Clapton next to Harrison,' said the director happily.

'Correct.'

'And look at the broads... On two.'

The camera picked up two black girls 'oh-oohing' together beside the platform, dressed like Delgado and Garfield in camouflage fatigues and berets with CLF patches.

'Jenny Bogle and Anastasia Rodriguez,' whispered the PA.

'Jesus Christ,' said the director, 'It's the concert for Cascara!'

Delgado snatched a glance behind him and sang as he had never sung before.

'You've taken our homes and our privacy

141

You've taken everything except
The sun and the sea...'

He could not believe the sound behind him. These were his heroes, capitalists maybe, some of them, one or two rumoured to be millionaires, but Delgado did not care. It was the happiest moment in his life. Revolution couldn't hold a candle to this. The music surrounded him and he sang his head off.

'I came here to ask you most humbly
Please won't you grant us our liberty
We want our Freedom
Give us our Freedom...'

And the delegates looked at their song-sheets translated into the language of each one of them, and sang along...

On Cascara it was Carnival again, everyone dancing to the rhythm. In the site office Miguel danced with Pepito while Pamela sat forward close to the screen.

The phone rang and Baxter picked it up.

'Baxter, it's Rob. Me and the guys want to offer our congratulations. Independence is a shoe-in.'

'Let's hope so,' said Baxter. 'It's looking good.'

'But I'm looking beyond the celebrations. I'm hoping that you guys and Spenco can soon resume the fruitful relationship that we previously enjoyed.'

'I don't think we can make any assumptions, Rob. It's a whole new ball game.'

There was a short silence then Rob began whispering and Baxter guessed that he was trying to be discreet. 'Hey, Baxter, you're still going to need people who understand advertising, marketing, distribution. I'm not married to Spenco. When this is over, why don't we have lunch.'

Baxter grinned, muttered a maybe into the phone and hung up. He looked down at Pamela who was perched by the TV set, the glow from it giving her an ethereal look.

'I think we can defuse those explosives now,' he said and made for the door.

'Be right with you,' she replied, singing along with Delgado.

'We want our Free-dom
Give us our Free-dom...'

Baxter waved to the crowd as he made his way to the rig and they waved back happily.

'We are a very poor people
And we're easily led
We have to scratch with our hands
To keep our babies fed
Now you bring in your soldiers
And put the gun to our head
The way things are going
We'd be better off dead...'

'We want our free-dom,' Baxter sang as he stooped beneath the legs of the rigs, unhooking the sticks of dynamite. They were redundant now. They had done their job and Delgado was doing the rest. 'Give us our free-dom,' he sang as he climbed the ladder onto the platform.

He was working fast, tongue out in concentration and at first did not see the soldier above him on the upper balcony of the platform, not until a bolt was dislodged and landed at his feet. He jumped back, startled, looked at it and up at the soles of two boots. Squinting to his left he saw the man fixing something to a stanchion. He frowned and tiptoed to the ladder, climbed it and got behind him. Baxter shivered with apprehension then saw his chance. A cable with a dog-clip hung by the man's side. Normally it was used for lifting barrels. Now it would have another function.

He tiptoed up to the man, held his breath, clipped the lead to his belt, hit the pulley button and stepped back as the man was lifted twenty feet to hang by his belt and twist slowly in the air.

Baxter stood back, saw a small, flat, magnetic disk explosive stuck to the stanchion. It had a timer and the seconds were ticking away. He placed his hands on his hips and looked up.

'Now then,' he said, 'What the hell are you...'

Then he was being grabbed by the shoulders and pulled backwards, spun round and slammed against the rail, a big man with foul breath holding him in a fierce grip, a forearm against Baxter's throat. Over his shoulder, twenty feet to the rear of the rig, Baxter could see a second explosive charge.

'Who are you?' Baxter wheezed. 'Why are you doing this?'

'For the bloodshed,' said Kessler. 'For the money. We are the dogs of war.'

'Who's paying you? It's the bloody French, isn't it? I can smell the garlic on your br...'

Then Kessler released him, stepped back, battered a short right-hander under Baxter's heart and ran, shouting over his shoulder to take cover. The explosives were set to blow in thirty seconds.

Baxter sagged against the rail then dragged himself upright, clutching his chest, fighting for breath, then held up an arm as he saw Pamela walking towards him, looking thoughtful.

From the loudspeakers came the sound of a standing ovation as Delgado's last chord faded, and the words of the commentator:

'In a rare moment of unanimity, the United Nations is today just that. Let us hope that today's vote to give Cascara independence will herald a new era of peace and prosperity for the island.'

Baxter staggered over to the bomb with Pamela behind him, wrenched it off and held it to his stomach, fighting the nausea.

'Baxter, I've been thinking,' Pamela said, looking seriously over his shoulder and nodding to herself. 'All I've been doing is to get back at Dad. But with good reason. He's a prick.'

Baxter wheezed, tapped her arm, held up the explosive. She gazed at it uncomprehendingly.

'Bomb,' he wheezed. 'Goes off in twenty seconds,' then turned her and pointed. Frowning, she walked towards the second explosive and touched it, then turned back to him, her face a question mark.

'Is this the bomb?'

Baxter nodded, held his hand up. 'Ten seconds,' he gasped then threw the thing like a frisbee away from him. At last she understood, ripped it off and threw. Baxter had a glimpse of her body, looking like a ballet dancer as the bomb sailed away, then there was a double explosion which sent him stumbling against the rig.

On the opposite cliff face, the mercenaries took their cue and pressed their plungers. Three simultaneous explosions blasted rock from the cliff and sent torrents of water spewing into the sea.

Baxter leant across the rail and watched, saw the waterfalls merge and become a river, like bloody Niagara, he thought, then he was conscious of someone behind him.

Kessler was nodding in satisfaction. 'The water is destroyed,' he said. 'The mission is accomplished.' He looked at Pamela as she came up to them, white-faced with shock. Kessler clicked his heels, reached into his pocket and turned to Baxter.

'If you ever have need of an army,' he said, 'here's my card.' He slipped it into Baxter's breast-pocket, saluted and was gone. Baxter blinked at Pamela. Behind them the loudspeakers were blasting out speeches of congratulations from the UN. In front of them, the mineral water flowed into the sea.

Independent and bankrupt in one fell swoop, he thought and sat down, feeling very sore and very old.

Eighteen

For a week Baxter did not leave the rig. He slept on it at night and fiddled with it by day, turning wheels, opening and closing stopcocks, but there was nothing. The cliff face opposite had long since urinated the last of the water and now the well was dry.

On the eighth day the others made their final plea to him, shouting up at him from the ground, telling him to come on down. It was a magnificent obsession, but it was pointless, and besides, he had to prepare for the ceremony, to accept formally the scroll of independence.

'It's time to go home, Baxter,' said Pamela.

'Face facts man,' said Eric, 'the water's gone.'

Baxter gripped the rail and looked down at them, willing them to see it his way.

'Look, when they activated this drill, they hit an underground well they didn't know about. The explosion may have caused some geological shift or fracture. There could be oceans of it still down there.'

'You've been telling us that for a week,' said Pepito.

'It could take a week,' Baxter protested. 'It could take a year.'

'It's not going to happen, Baxter,' said Delgado, and there was something in his voice that made Baxter want to cry. Delgado was right. They were all right. He was the daft one. He'd been thinking like Delgado once thought. They're all out of step but our Jock.

He sighed and climbed down the ladder. Pamela kissed him and pulled him away and they walked from the rig,

146

up the track towards the town.

'They only gave us independence because they knew we had nothing of value,' Baxter said.

'At least everything we don't have is ours,' said Garfield, trying to cheer him up.

'We've been offered a record deal,' said Delgado.

Pepito grunted at him. 'I hardly think your royalties will pay the national debt.'

'I've been seeing a lot of bats,' said Pamela.

Baxter stared at her. 'So?'

'The excrement of bats is guano,' she explained, 'the richest fertiliser in the world. One day it could be a valuable export.'

But Baxter would not be comforted. 'How do the people eat while we wait for the bats to crap?' he asked and there was nothing more to add.

They walked on in silence then Eric stopped, the first one to hear it, a strange whistling sound turning into a low rumble.

'What's that noise?' he asked.

'With our luck, it's probably the volcano,' Baxter grumbled, and for a moment they thought he was right. The earth shook and Pamela grabbed Baxter's hand as they turned and gazed in the direction of the rig.

It seemed to be moving, as if something was shaking it, then there was a roar, like a breaker crashing on pebbles, amplified a thousand times, and a jet of liquid spurted sixty feet. This time it wasn't water. It was black.

Baxter looked at Pamela and saw that his prayers had been answered. The word 'oil' bubbled on her lips and her eyes shone with delight. Suddenly she was her father's daughter again.

Nineteen

Independence Day dawned hot and windy. By noon a gale was blowing off the sea and the Union Jack on the flag-pole by the jetty came down reluctantly, straining against the wind. No one cheered but the cameras of the world's Press clicked and whirred, recording the moment for posterity. The square was packed as never before, the Cascarans mingling with reporters and TV crews. All morning the people had been giving interviews, trying to answer the standard question – how did it feel to be part of a group with one of the highest per capita incomes in the world? And no one knew the answer.

Then the band struck up with the Cascaran national anthem as the new flag was raised; a blue and white flag showing the bows of a ship going down into the ocean. It had been designed by Baxter and he saluted it proudly. For the occasion he had dressed in cricket flannels and a double-breasted yachting blazer. To his right, Delgado and Garfield stood in freshly laundered fatigues, singing along with the anthem.

Then it was over and Pepito handed the neatly folded Union Jack to Delgado who, in turn, handed it to Baxter.

'I think you've earned this privilege, Foreign Secretary,' said Delgado.

'Thank you, Mister President,' said Baxter, then turned and walked a few feet along the jetty to where Sir Malcolm stood, glowering. Silently Baxter handed over the flag.

'The rope also belongs to Britain, Thwaites,' he snapped.

'Then you shall have it, sir,' said Baxter, waving Pepito across.

'There goes lunch,' said Delgado, and Garfield grinned.

The cameras clicked. Sir Malcolm looked nervously at his watch and over his shoulder at the naval cutter moored at the end of the jetty, then he was being nudged by Baxter.

'Smile, Sir Malcolm, as the cameras catch the dying moments of a British colony.'

'The dying moments of my career, you mean,' he said, smiling like a gargoyle. 'Thanks to this disastrous episode, the Right Honourable Margaret Thatcher is going to have my balls.'

At this, there was a blast of the ship's siren and they turned to see Dolores waving.

'If the PM doesn't, Sir Malcolm,' said Baxter, 'then Dolores certainly will.'

Sir Malcolm shuddered, slapped the scroll of independence into Baxter's hand and scuttled off down the jetty without a word of farewell.

Then the band struck up again. Reggae this time, and the singing and dancing began. Baxter turned and felt himself being grabbed by Pamela and a young, very pregnant Creole. As he swayed to the rhythm, he gazed happily at the throng of Cascarans and wondered if wealth would change them.

He didn't know, but it was a nice problem to have.

BACHELOR BOYS

THE YOUNG ONES'

BOOK

BEN ELTON · LISE MAYER · RIK MAYALL

Call it bad karma or anarchy in the U.K., there's never
been anything quite like the cult-hit T.V. series *The
Young Ones* — totally bizarre, totally original, totally
aggressive and . . . totally TOTAL. So, here are the
Young Ones in their own write at last: Rick the Radical
Poet, Vyvyan the Psychopathic Punk, Neil the Suicidal
Hippy, and Mike, the Would-Be Spiv. Together they
reveal The Ultimate Truth About Everything to their avid
fans, including absolutely zillions of helpless hints on:

★ HOBBIES
Neil's 101 really interesting things to do with a tea-cup
★ FILTH
Some kissing hints from Vyvyan. Lesson one: Snog the Dog
★ LAUGHS
Including Rick's only joke: These are my pants and I'm sticking to
them!!!
PLUS
a controversial statement from the Acne Liberation Front. The
Young Ones say: WEAR YOUR SPOTS WITH PRIDE

NON-FICTION/HUMOUR   0 7221 5765 7   £2.95

The Completely Draining Experience

UP THE CISTERN

**A lavish
celebration of
the smallest
room**

JAMES RIDDLE

A wind in the ear of all you big spenders, who pass on average at least six days a year closeted away – you can all come out now; you'll never need to feel non-loo again! Relief at last, in this penetrating exploration of the Great British Obsession. Relax (and discover):

* WHAT happens if you cover the loo-pan with cling film and wait for the unsuspecting user to create a stink
* WHO said 'The evil that men do lives after them'
* IF you're ready to blast off for the executive toilet, or always bogged down on the outside, waiting for life's 'ENGAGED' sign to become 'VACANT'

PLUS

piles of other banal retentions, loophemisms and moving verses

IN

The only book guaranteed to put bums back on seats – and fill every loo in the land!

COMPLETELY EXPURGATED VERSION

NON-FICTION/HUMOUR   0 7221 7350 4   £1.75

TERRY AND ARTHUR ARE STILL IN BUSINESS

Minder

– back again

Anthony Masters

Terry McCann and Arthur Daley are the Laurel and Hardy of
London's criminal fraternity. Arthur's the one with the silver
tongue, he could talk his way past St. Peter at the pearly gates
if he wanted to. They say he even charges his mum petrol
money when he runs her home . . . And when Arthur's hot air
finally blows cold, it's usually poor old Terry who's left to do
the dirty work! If there's ever a fast buck to be made, they'll be
there like a shot. The only trouble is, where Terry and Arthur
are concerned, there's always a sting in the tale as well!

MINDER – BACK AGAIN is based on the smash hit Thames
Television series created by Leon Griffiths, starring Dennis
Waterman and George Cole.

TV TIE-IN/FICTION   0 7221 5823 8   £1.50

Also by Anthony Masters, available in Sphere paperback:

MINDER

A selection of bestsellers from SPHERE

FICTION

THE SEA CAVE	Alan Scholefield	£2.25 ☐
THE JUDAS CODE	Derek Lambert	£2.25 ☐
MONIMBO	Arnaud de Borchgrave and Robert Moss	£2.25 ☐
KING OF DIAMONDS	Carolyn Terry	£2.50 ☐
AUTUMN TIGER	Bob Langley	£1.95 ☐

FILM & TV TIE-INS

WEMBLEY FRAGGLE GETS THE STORY	Deborah Perlberg	£1.50 ☐
MAROONED IN FRAGGLE ROCK	David Young	£1.50 ☐
THE DOOZER DISASTER	Michaela Muntean	£1.75 ☐
ONCE UPON A TIME IN AMERICA	Lee Hays	£1.75 ☐
THE DUNE STORYBOOK	Joan Vinge	£2.50 ☐

NON-FICTION

THE COMPLETE HANDBOOK OF PREGNANCY	Wendy Rose-Neil	£5.95 ☐
THE STORY OF THE SHADOWS	Mike Read	£2.95 ☐
WHO'S REALLY WHO	Compton Miller	£2.95 ☐
WORST MOVIE POSTERS OF ALL TIME	Greg Edwards	£4.95 ☐
THE STOP SMOKING DIET	Jane Ogle	£1.50 ☐

All Sphere books are available at your local bookshop or newsagent, or can be ordered direct from the publisher. Just tick the titles you want and fill in the form below.

Name_____

Address_____

_____

Write to Sphere Books, Cash Sales Department, P.O. Box 11, Falmouth, Cornwall TR10 9EN

Please enclose cheque or postal order to the value of the cover price plus:

UK: 55p for the first book, 22p for the second and 14p per copy for each additional book ordered to a maximum charge of £1.75.

OVERSEAS: £1.00 for the first book and 25p for each additional book.

BFPO & EIRE: 55p for the first book, 22p for the second book plus 14p per copy for the next 7 books, thereafter 8p per book.

Sphere Books reserve the right to show new retail prices on covers which may differ from those previously advertised in the text or elsewhere, and to increase postal rates in accordance with the PO.